Knock Socks Off!

KING EDWARD'S JUNIOR SCHOOL

Cover illustration by Fleur Smailes.
Title page illustration by Angus Cannock.

Published by Squawk Books.

Copyright © 2014 retained by contributors.

All rights reserved. No part of this book may be used or reproduced in any manner without the written permission of the publisher, contributor or King Edward's Junior School.

All characters in this anthology are fictitious and any resemblance to actual persons, living or dead, is entirely coincidental.

ISBN 978-0-9571300-4-3

Introduction by Mr Greg Taylor, Headmaster, King Edward's Junior School.

As you sit back immersing yourself in this unique, stylish and very individual masterpiece, please contemplate what an amazing piece of modern day literature it actually is. But more than that; the works are all produced by our talented and imaginative children from King Edward's Junior School, Bath.

The enormous pleasure this book will bring and the joy you get in reading the variety of pieces is only surpassed by the sheer delight the children have had in writing and illustrating it. I pay tribute to their flair, creativity, their grasp of language and use of prose.

Knock your socks off! does exactly what it says on the tin! It is a magnificent, mind-boggling array of children's work. I thank the young authors for their commitment, determination and effort, and the staff for their input, advice and support. A special thank you goes to Mrs Donovan and Mrs MacFarlan for the hours spent bringing this initial (some might say crazy) idea to fruition. Well done to everyone. You all should be extremely proud of the result; a published book. Have much fun reading!

This book is dedicated to James MacFarlan, for thirty-seven years of inspired teaching, which twenty-three years of KEJS children have enjoyed.

Illustration by Wilfred Saumarez-Smith

Classes: 3L and 3J
The Magic of Language

Illustration by Megan Pike

In Year 3 we have been experimenting with the wonderful world of language, thinking about how to choose our words carefully to make the greatest impact. Haikus provide the perfect opportunity to do this; the short, three line structure, with its 5-7-5 pattern of syllables means that we have to make every word count.

We also tried to be inventive with language when writing our question poems. We combined the 'wh' words which we had been learning about in spelling lessons and the punctuation we had been practising in grammar lessons with our own original, creative ideas.

When we read extracts from novels by C. S. Lewis and Roald Dahl, in which children were magically sucked into pictures, we wondered what that might feel like. We decided to have a go at writing about it ourselves. We hope you will enjoy reading the results.

Illustration by Edward Lewis

Questions
Ned Alcock

Eagle, where did you get your beautiful beak?
I yanked it from an eye-catching parrot with lots of magical colours.

Meadow Haiku
Ned Alcock

Tall, waving, green grass.
Big, orange sun shining bright.
Tops of trees waving.

Questions
Jay Bardsley

Polar bear, where did you discover your white fur?
I stole it from the white snow.

Meadow Haiku
Jay Bardsley

I saw trees swaying,
The wind blowing the dead leaves,
Over bright, green grass.

Questions
Freddy Blofeld

Manta ray, where did you discover your spectacular wings?
I borrowed them from a low flying Easyjet!

Meadow Haiku
Freddy Blofeld

Busy bees buzzing,

I hear loud sirens wailing,

Planes high in the sky.

Questions
Josie Butters

Panda, where did you find those black patches around your big eyes?
I stole them from the captain of a pirate ship.
Wolf, where did you find those sharp teeth?
I discovered some hanging icicles and put them in my mouth.

Meadow Haiku
Josie Butters

Leaves falling
off trees.
Plants growing
in the green
grass.
Small birds
flying high.

Questions
Tobin Bye

Kitten, where did you find your glittering, small eyes?
I found them in the glistening reflection of the silver stars on the surface of a lake.

Scorpion, where did you discover your deadly poison in the tip of your black tail?
I stole it from a slithering snake's hissing mouth.

Meadow Haiku
Tobin Bye

I see fluffy clouds,
The wasps collecting nectar.
I hear birds talking.

Questions
Zac Grosjean

Skunk, how did you get a deadly stench in your tail?
I fell in a dustbin full of sour milk and rubbed my tail around it.

Meadow Haiku
Zac Grosjean

Clouds high in the sky.
Hovering wasps in the sky.
Small birds in the sky.

Questions
George Lowrie

Giraffe, where did you get your enormous neck?
I captured an elephant and dragged it into a marsh and took its trunk.

Meadow Haiku
George Lowrie

Busy bees flying.
Wind blowing the leaves on the trees,
Weeds, small weeds growing.

Questions
Henry Jones

Tiger snake, where did you find your dark, patterned scales?
I strangled them from a zebra.
Sausage dog, where did you get your cylindrical body?
I stole it from a big hot dog sign at a crowded fair.

Meadow Haikus
Henry Jones

Small, green grass blowing.
Branches swaying left and right.
Orange leaves falling.

Big trees, swaying slow.
Tiny, curly, wooden roots.
Little birds chirping.

Questions
Charlotte Laver

Elephant, where did you discover those massive, long, grey tusks?
I found them in a gold chest under the trees in the jungle.

Meadow Haiku
Charlotte Laver

I hear birds singing.
Brown, orange, red leaves falling.
Hot, shining, red sun.

Questions
Edward Lewis

Elephant, where did you find those gigantic ears?
I stole them from a woman's enormous purse.

Meadow Haiku
Edward Lewis

I saw views of Bath,
The annoying small midges.
I hear people talk.

Questions
Wilfie Mantell-Jacob

Centipede, where did you find your hundred legs?

I found them in a tiny treasure chest, resting in the dark.

Hedgehog, where did you find your shimmering, sharp spikes?

I found them under a giant pine needle tree, covered in snow.

Meadow Haikus
Wilfie Mantell-Jacob

Houses standing tall.
Small twigs falling from the trees.
Dry mud on the ground.

Floating soft feathers.
Miniature stones on brown mud.
Quiet buzzing insects.

Questions
Kit McKeever

Rattlesnake, where did you find the beautiful patterns on your back?
I pinched them from a schoolboy's patterned tie.

Meadow Haiku
Kit McKeever

Tall, waving, thin grass.
Standing in the sloppy mud.
Great to play football.

Questions
Douglas Pritchard

Grasshopper, why are you bright green?
I rolled in the chopped leaves of mint sauce.

Meadow Haiku
Douglas Pritchard

Big planes in the sky.
Big leaves blowing in the wind.
Red berries falling.

Questions
Rory Medley

Parrot, where did you find those coloured feathers?

I pulled them from a sparkling rainbow behind the gleaming sun.

Great white shark, where did you find those sharp teeth?

I found them behind a waterfall in an ice palace.

Meadow Haikus
Rory Medley

The wind in the sky.

Houses with their fires on.

Berries on the ground.

Cars stuck in traffic.

A creepy, crawly spider.

The church bell ringing.

Questions
Alfie Myers

Emperor Tamarin, how did you find such a fine, curly moustache?
I stole it from a remote igloo at the North Pole one Christmas Eve.
Pig, where did you get that little pig tail from?
I yanked the spring from the most bouncy pogo-stick and dyed it pink.
Hedgehog, where did you find your prickly spikes?
I accidentally ran into a green cactus.

Meadow Haiku
Alfie Myers

I see shining sun.
I hear the wind rustling trees.
Birds singing quietly.

Questions
Megan Pike

Zebra, where did you find your beautiful, black and white stripes?
I pinched them from an old treasure chest filled with scrunched up pirate flags left on the beach.
Tiger, where did you discover your black stripes?
They were carved on my fur by the sticky, black mud from the flooding River Nile.

Meadow Haikus
Megan Pike

Green refreshing grass.
White clouds floating in the sky.
Sun shining brightly.

Ripening red berries.
Damp, squelchy mud, grass growing.
Bath shining brightly.

The Ship Picture
Thomas Moir

As I walked down the gallery I saw a picture of a ship on a stormy sea. I stared at it, touched it and then carried on walking with my eyes closed. Just then, I felt something pulling me. I felt terrified! I tried to run but my feet felt like lead. A shiver ran down my spine and I was shaking all over. Suddenly I realised that I was in the picture! I ran and ran but someone or something was pulling me back! I could hear crashing waves and the smell of the salty sea. I turned around to find a pirate staring straight at me!

Apples
Thomas Moir

Green and rosy red.
All shapes, sizes and colours,
Growing day and night.

Questions
Jasper Nejad

Snake, where did you get your strong muscles?

I stole them from a wondrous whale's tail.

Spider, where did you get your long, sharp fangs?

I grabbed them from the tooth of a great white shark.

Bear, how did you get your brown, bushy fur?

I plucked it from the bark of a tree in a wizard's garden.

Hyena, where did you get your evil laugh?

I snatched it from the jaws of a cackling witch.

Raspberries
Jasper Nejad

Juicy raspberries,

They grow in the garden.

Soft, squishy red gems.

Questions
Harvey Newsam

Snake, where did you get your slithery scales?
I grabbed them from the shiny pebbles under the water.
Snake, where did you get your dagger-like tongue?
I ripped it off an elf's red hat.
Shark, where did you get your dirty teeth?
I stole them from a muddy soldier's filthy mace.
Tarantula, where did you get your furry body?
I plucked it from a lazy tiger's paw, as he slept under an old oak tree.

Apples
Harvey Newsam

Shining in the sun,
Soon getting squashed into pies.
Juicy, red apples.

Questions
Ben Phillips

Tiger, how did you get your eye-catching claws?

I stole the teeth of a great white shark.

Polar bear, where did you get that warm fur?

I won it in a battle with a fierce tiger.

Jaguar, how did you get your incredible speed?

I ate a fast car in my sleep.

Tortoise, how did you get your incredibly hard shell?

I made it from a dead elephant's bones.

Apples
Ben Phillips

Sweet apples growing.

Apples, lovely and juicy.

Always love apples.

Questions
Isobel Reid

Tiger, where did you get your dark black stripes?
I burnt them in a magical, forest fire.
Where did you get your long, see-through whiskers?
I stole them from a freaky, giant cat as it ran past me.
How did you get your magnificent, long tail?
I found it in a high, bendy tree on a wizard's farm.
How did you get your bright, orange fur?
I borrowed it from the scary wizard's hat.
How did you get your glittery eyes?
I begged and begged for them from a princess' castle.

Lemons
Isobel Reid

Delicious lemons,
Juicy but sour yellow.
Nice to have on fish.

Questions
Freddie Russell

Green Pit Viper, where did you get your gleaming, green body?

I stole it from the grass in a magic forest.

Blue shark, where did you get your sharp teeth?

I stole them from a magic swordfish in a cave deep in the ocean.

King Cobra, where did you get your venom?

I won a bet against an evil elf that I met in a magical cave.

Tomatoes
Freddie Russell

Sweet, red tomatoes.

Size of kumquats, taste of joy.

I love tomatoes.

Questions
Orson Savage

Tiger, where did you find your super stripes?

I discovered them in a secret cave behind a tropical waterfall.

Elephant, where did you get your gigantic tusks?

I won them from an enormous megalodon.

Rhino, where did you find those spiky horns?

I stole them from a rainbow unicorn.

Praying mantis, where did you get your sharp, green arms?

A wizard made them from his sharpened axe.

Ladybird, where did you find your dark, black spots?

I collected them from the skin of a fierce killer whale.

Cabbages
Orson Savage

Fresh green cabbages.

Caterpillars munching leaves.

Lovely cabbages.

Questions
Oscar Shonfeld

Tortoise, where did you get your hard, leathery shell?
I captured it from an elephant's mighty tusks.
Spider, where did you get your fine, silky web?
I absorbed it from the dazzling dew that covered the fantastic, green grass.
Crab, where did you get your crushing claws?
I stole them from a blacksmith elf's great hammer.
Rattlesnake, where did you get your excruciating venom?
I sucked it cautiously from a wizard's smoking cauldron.

Tomatoes
Oscar Shonfeld

Juicy tomatoes.
Glorious, succulent, red
Spheres of delight.

The Desert Picture
Oscar Shonfeld

As I glanced at the desert picture, everything seemed to be moving. The sand was blowing, the camels were walking and I wondered what could be going on.

All of a sudden I felt an extraordinary force sucking me towards the picture. I was terrified. I didn't know what to do. I turned away from the painting and ran and screamed for help, but something kept pulling me backwards. Who knows what was pulling me back, but whatever it was, it was very, very strong.

I felt the scorching sun beating down on me and sand blowing into my eyes. The crumbling sand was pouring into my shoes like liquid. When I looked ahead, instead of a room with furniture, all I saw was bare desert. As I stayed there for a minute or two I realised something ...

I WAS IN THE PICTURE!

Questions
Ben Sim

Shark, where did you get your sharp teeth?
I carved them out of the moon.
Rattlesnake, where did you get your rattle?
I ate a Hawaiian maraca.
Jellyfish, where did you get your long, stinging tentacles?
I grabbed them from Medusa's head, while she slept in her lair of statues.
Otter, where did you get your addiction for shiny things?
A beam of light shot out of the moon and hit me.
Cheetah, where did you get your distinctive spots?
I pinched them from an ogre's dice.
Tiger, where did you get your black stripes?
I got burnt in a raging forest fire.

Apples
Ben Sim

Red tender apple,
Juicy, bursting with flavour.
Crumble time, picked plump.

Questions
Max Stein

Shark, where did you get your sharp, shiny teeth?
I stole them from a giant tiger, sleeping in the sun.
Snake, where did you get your shiny scales?
I stole them from the stars on a wizard's pointy hat.
Tree, where did you get your rough, green leaves?
I plucked them from the grass in an enchanted garden.
Crocodile, where did you get your leathery skin?
I bought it from a gigantic elephant that was passing by.

Lemons
Max Stein

Shiny smooth lemon,
Hanging waiting to be picked.
Yellow, waxy fruit.

The Picture
Toby Swale

That night as I lay in my bed a gentle breeze blew on my face. I opened my eyes and felt a big force pulling me towards the picture hanging above my head. It would not stop. As I struggled to get away from the force, the more I was pulled by it. My head and shoulders were being sucked into the picture and my body was being recreated inside it.

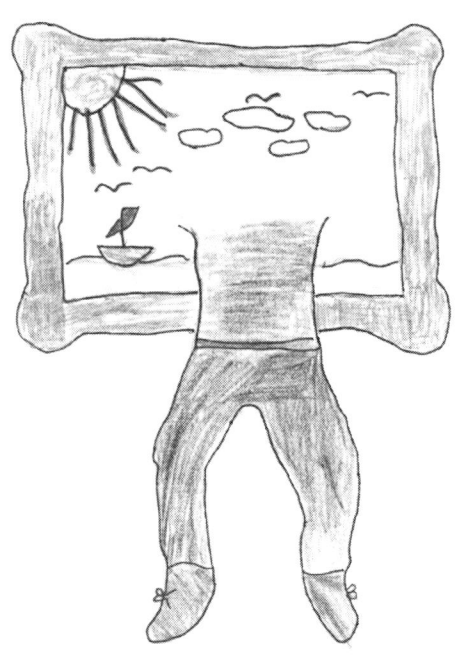

Then a flash of light surrounded me and suddenly my surroundings changed.

There was a calm lake. The trees covered the light from the sun. I felt the same gentle breeze. Behind a brick wall a bunch of people with big guns were shouting, 'We're here, we're here!'

They bowed at me as if I was their master. Four men came with a big chair and covered it for me. I stood there, thinking. I felt nervous, but then I worked out that they were policemen, protecting me. The road led up to a beautiful castle.

'Whose is this?' I asked.

'It's yours,' they said.

I was speechless.

Carrots
Toby Swale

Juicy ripe carrots,

Freshly picked from damp soil.

Bright orange delights.

Questions
George Tinworth

Rat, where did you get your large, sharp teeth?

I found them in a mystical cavern.

Wolf cub, where did you find your dark, fluffy fur?

I won it from a fierce witch's cat.

Red tiger, how do you survive the cold?

I caught glaring sunbeams and put them in my coat.

Plums
George Tinworth

Round, gorgeous big plums.

Chickens love the juicy fruit,

Falling from the tree.

The Fox
Zoe Trezies

The fox's white teeth glistened in the darkness. The animal prowled over to me until it was only centimetres away. It caught my leg. Its strength was incredible. I yanked my foot hard and the fox lost its grip. I ran as fast as I could to the house. I looked back. The fox's sharp, white teeth were still shining in the moonlight!

Corn
Zoe Trezies

Waiting to be picked,

Hiding from the scorching sun.

Tall and golden corn.

Questions
Harry Tweedale

Jaguar, how did you get your impressive speed?
I stole it from the wind as it pushed me along.
Crocodile, how did you get your glinting teeth?
I stole them from a terrifying great white shark.
King Cobra, how did you get your amazing scales?
I plucked them from a spider with eight glimpsing eyes.
Octopus, how did you get your piercing tentacles?
I snatched them from a bristly caterpillar.

Apples
Harry Tweedale

Shivering apples,

Not wanting to be gathered,

Hide in the branches.

Questions
Claudia Williams

Tiger, how did you get your orange and black, stripy fur?
I collected it from the dark, black, ugly duckling and a furry orang-utan.
Frog, how did you get your froggy feet?
I begged for them from the secret sea of doom.
Ladybird, how did you get your polka-dot spots?
I snatched them from the fierce jaguar who stalks through the woods.
Duck, how did you get your bright, yellow feathers?
I pinched them from a mean giant's sun.

Golden Wheat
Claudia Williams

Golden wheat waving.
Farmers collecting it to make
Crusty, hot, brown bread.

Questions
Elise Withey

Fox, where did you get your russet-coloured fur?

I stole it from the autumn leaves, which crunched beneath my paws.

Oyster, how did you get your pearl?

I snatched it from a mermaid's purse.

Butterfly, where did you discover your vibrant colours?

I borrowed them from the crock of gold at the end of the rainbow.

Kitten, how did you get your fluffy coat?

I caught the soft, silky thistledown, blowing in the summer breeze.

Parrot, how did you learn to talk?

A magician from the seventh sun taught me.

The Stormy Sea Picture (an extract)

I was walking in a gallery when a painting suddenly caught my eye. It was a painting of a giant ship. There was something odd about that picture. I shivered and hurried on. Weirdly, I felt an urge to return to the canvas. To my amazement, the people on the deck were moving! I could hear seagulls calling and waves crashing and I could smell the salty sea spray. I tried to fight an invisible force, but it was too strong for me and I felt myself being sucked into the picture. I disappeared into a whirlwind of sparkles! I was so scared that I could almost hear my heart pounding. My mouth was dry and the last thing I remembered was thinking, 'The label on the picture!' before I lost consciousness.

The next thing I felt was a bucket of water being poured onto my head. Ugh, salty seawater! I coughed and spluttered, looked up and saw one of the people from the painting.

Finally came the time I was dreading; the time to meet the captain. I walked into his cabin.

'Sit down!' said a gruff voice.

I looked at the captain. He had a black, bushy beard and dark, beetle-like eyes. Give him an eye patch and a parrot and he could have been straight out of *Treasure Island*! He even had a wooden leg!

'Who permitted you to land on my ship?'

'Errrr,' I stammered. 'What is your ship called?'

'It's the Titanic, the greatest ship on the seas.'

My blood ran cold. I had to get out of there fast!

Class: 4R

Much of the writing by 4R stems from our enthusiastic study of Roald Dahl's *Matilda*. So here are fearsome and sadistic teachers, strange-looking and frightening to their pupils. There are sarcastic and cruel school reports, of the kind teachers at Crunchem Hall might write.

Alongside these, a few children have written short stories as part of a challenge to produce works of 500 words or fewer. Their imagination soars far and wide...

Illustration by Cameron Finnigan

Illustration by Max Dennis

The Monster
Harry Adams

Once upon a time there was a little village called Batheaston. There was a church, a school and two shops. The people who lived there were very happy. But there was something wrong about it. There was a little boy called Bill and he was frightened because it was Halloween.

Bill did not like going trick or treating because he was scared he might bump into zombies going into people's houses for sweets.

His mum said, 'Bed time, Bill.'

When he was in bed and all the lights were out, he heard some footsteps. What would he do? His mum and dad were asleep.

The footsteps were getting closer to his room. He pulled the duvet over his head, but he could hear the footsteps growing louder and louder! He was shaking with fear. Then he felt something touch him.

'Hello, who is there?' he asked.

'Meow meow.'

It was his cat, Maisie. Phew!

Mr Hardthorn's First Day
Anastasia Andreou

The door opened and in staggered Mr Hardthorn. He was very old and moved slowly and quietly as he walked across the classroom. He had thin legs like twigs and small eyes like peas. His hair was unkempt and riddled with nits. He was wearing an old brown cardigan that had a big hole at the back. His orange corduroy trousers were full of coffee stains and his white ankle socks had turned black.

As Mr Hardthorn read out the register a little boy called Henry Droolspit started to laugh. Henry was the naughtiest boy in the class. He was seven-years-old and had a long, pointy nose like a carrot. He was naughty because he always got into fights with other children and also liked to make fun of the teachers.

'Who's laughing in my classroom!' shouted Mr Hardthorn.

Suddenly all the children in the classroom fell silent, except for Henry who was laughing like mad.

Mr Hardthorn slowly crept up behind Henry's desk and whipped his hands hard with a long, sharp cane.

'YELP!' cried Henry in pain.

'Why were you laughing in my classroom?' said

Mr Hardthorn angrily.

'I'm laughing at your ridiculous clothes,' said Henry in a brave voice.

'That's it! You will now spend lunch time on toilet duty,' said Mr Hardthorn.

Toilet duty was a disgusting punishment that teachers gave to young children when they were exceptionally naughty in class. The children were given a slippery soap and a small sponge to clean all the teachers' toilets.

While Henry was cleaning the toilets he had an idea. His plan was to put super glue on the toilets so the teachers would stick to them when they sat down.

A few hours later, the children heard Mr Hardthorn screaming in the men's toilets.

'I'm stuck, I'm stuck!' he screamed. 'Who is responsible for this?'

Crunchem Hall Reports
James Bassil

Dear Mr and Mrs Simpson,

Did you know that bats are actually blind and that they use sound to know where they are? Your son Bart is like a bat, but without the sense of sound. He bangs into things, people, tables and chairs. In fact he bangs into almost everything. My suggestion is to get glasses or contact lenses.

Sincerely,

Bart's teacher

Dear Mr and Mrs Greece,

Did you know that elephants can weigh up to four tonnes? Your daughter Ella stomps around the school like an elephant, causing books to fall off the shelves, and when she's running, making the cabinets topple over. My suggestion is to eat less or eat more healthy things.

Sincerely,

Ella's teacher

Mr Thorndusk's First Day
Erica Baxter

The door opened and in glided Mr Thorndusk. His feet moved across the hall floor as though it was ice. All the children backed away. He was wearing a bright pink jacket with green buttons and a purple, yellow and blue-patterned tie. His shoes were fluorescent orange riding boots. He slunk into Class Four ready for registration, sat down and looked at the class. He pointed at a small girl in the first row.

'You there in the first row. What's your name?'

'Isabella Down, Mr Thorndusk.'

'Stand up now class and sit down again. Now it's registration. Florence Swine?'

'Yes, Mr Thorndusk.'

'Elsie Thwipp?'

'It's Thripp, not Thwipp,' replied Elsie hastily.

'WHERE'S YOUR HOMEWORK DIARY?' bellowed Mr Thorndusk.

Elsie gave it to him, feebly.

'That's a break time in the cupboard, Elsie.'

'Yes sir,' Elsie replied.

'Class, go and get your pencil cases. We're going to have a spelling test. Ready? Please spell antidisestablishmentarianism. Now spell buccaneer.'

The children did the best they could with the spellings. Every single one was difficult.

'That will do for today, class. I'll mark them out of ten,' he muttered menacingly, his eyes glinting evilly.

'You've all got bad marks, so you'd better scarper before I get you with my cane,' he cackled fiendishly.

At that moment, every child in the classroom ran as fast as a cheetah at full pelt, down the corridor, out of the door, onto the meadow and back home again.

Mr Thorndusk went home whistling happily, hoping that tomorrow would be just as fun for him as today had been.

Mr Eagleshade's First Day
Ruairi Brady

The door opened and in flew Mr Eagleshade. His eyes were like a bird of prey. 'Good morning class, today we are going to do dissection,' he said.

The whole class gasped, except a boy called Tommy who said, 'Yes! What will we be dissecting?'

'A rat!' replied Mr Eagleshade with an evil glint in his eyes.

'I'm not feeling very well,' said a boy and he ran out of the classroom.

'COME BACK HERE!' raged Mr Eagleshade.

No-one wanted to be on the wrong side of him, so the boy came back to the classroom to find Mr Eagleshade had given five people detentions.

To the whole class's horror they found out they would be dissecting a *live* rat! Its eyes were like lasers. A girl nearly fainted because it was so ugly.

The rat looked at the class and then buried its teeth into the teacher's hand.

Mr Eagleshade jumped back, letting go of the rat, and it scuttled out of the room. Mr Eagleshade chased after it. The children thought it was an asinine thing to do and laughed.

Report for Crunchem Hall School
Max Brine

A great white shark is one of the most dangerous sea creatures in the world. Your son Jamie is very dangerous down in the science lab because he spills everything he holds, like the most dangerous chemicals in the school.

The Ghosts and the Asteroid
Angus Cannock

Jack Lemming was an ordinary school boy, mousey brown hair, skinny, freckles and scraped knees, but he had one blue and one brown eye, and wore a monocle because he was short-sighted in the blue eye. His hobby was star-gazing.

One afternoon, whilst doing his maths at home he felt a light tapping sensation on his shoulder, then a tingling as what felt like a hand went through his arm.

'Drat!' exclaimed a voice behind him, 'I wish my hand didn't go through things.'

Jack spun on his chair. 'Who's that? Get off me!' He noticed a translucent figure, but he didn't feel too scared. 'Albert Einstein?' he spluttered.

When the figure replied, 'Yes,' Jack fainted. Coming round he saw Einstein and Isaac Newton gazing down at him.

'Are you all right?' asked Einstein, concerned.

'I think not,' said Jack, fainting again.

'Wake up, Jack! Did aliens abduct you and beam you back?' asked Tommy, his friend.

'I saw Newton's and Einstein's ghosts!' Jack gabbled.

Jack's mother called them, 'Dinner's ready!'

'Jack was abducted by aliens. They've just beamed him back!' shouted Tommy.

'Well, beam downstairs. Your pizza's getting cold.'

'We'll talk later,' said Jack, dizzily.

Back in Jack's room, Tommy was speechless as the ghosts re-materialised.

'We need your help. Point your telescope over there,' said Newton, gesturing towards the window.

Jack saw an asteroid heading for Earth.

'It'll hit a school in Australia in seven days. You MUST warn them!' said Einstein. 'The astronomer Dr Brian May is in your village saving badgers. He'll help,' said Newton.

Dr May listened to Jack and contacted the Australian Prime Minister, who was a Queen fan!

The school was evacuated before the asteroid hit and all the children were saved. Jack was given a medal and a trip to Australia. He didn't tell anyone about the ghosts, but Einstein and Newton often visited him to discuss physics!

Crunchem Hall Visits the National Gallery
Wilf Clark

'Come on you maggots!' Miss Trunchbull boomed.

'It's cold,' someone screamed.

'Who said that?' the Trunchbull boomed.

'It's Angus,' Frank said, looking at the entrance.

'Right, now that we're in the National Gallery, it's off to Chokey. Wait! Where is the Chokey room?' Miss Trunchbull shrieked.

'There isn't one,' the person at the counter said softly.

'How can you not have a Chokey room!' the Trunchbull exclaimed.

'Did you know that this ceiling is over one hundred years old,' Matilda said to Lavender.

'Wow,' Miss Trunchbull said sarcastically.

'That was mean, wasn't it?' Matilda whispered to Lavender.

'Yes it was,' Lavender replied.

Then Miss Trunchbull touched a painting and it fell on her head. 'It was you Angus!' she splurted out. 'Right, as soon as we get back, it's off to the Chokey for you!'

'This painting is amazing because it's of me,' Miss

Trunchbull exclaimed. 'Maggots, we're going to look at this for a long time, but don't touch it or it's Chokey time!'

Then Tom tripped and touched Miss Trunchbull's painting and it snapped in two.

'Oh no!' Tom shouted. He shivered as Miss Trunchbull towered over him.

'Right, you're off to Chokey when we get back!'

Lord Lightningcloud's First Day
Alastair Claydon

The door burst open and in stormed Lord Lightningcloud. His beetle-black eyes darted around the classroom. He looked like a bull. His very wide body nearly didn't fit in the chair. His legs looked like logs.

Lord Lightningcloud taught P.E. He ordered the children to go to the meadow and take a station each. Every station had a gate; on the right was a selection of guns. Then Lord Lightningcloud arrived. He told them to pick up the AAP-E pistol.

'You're going to hit the targets and if you don't, it's the arm-breaker for you!' he said. 'Start!'

Twenty two out of twenty three children hit all the targets. One person, named Dean Thomas, hit none. Dean was a very thin boy. He had dark, black hair that was quite untidy at the back.

The arm-breaker was a weird machine. It had a bench and two rollers used to stretch the child's body. Just as Lord Lightningcloud was putting Dean on 'the machine', Miss Trunchbull came out of the school.

For the children that was the worst thing that

could happen. But for the teacher it was the best because Miss Trunchbull hated children, and they knew she'd support any punishment. The teacher went to meet her and they had a forty five minute conversation.

By the time they arrived back at the meadow, Dean had called the Police.

Lady Wormtree's First Day
Max Dennis

The door opened and in stomped Lady Wormtree with her chest puffed out like a robin. She had two earrings that were pale green and yellow. They were very ugly and suited her as she wasn't very pretty either. She was dressed in green breeches, a shirt and a checked jacket that didn't match anything else she wore. She looked really ugly and the children tried not to giggle, but then one little girl called Gertrude laughed out loud. Lady Wormtree looked Gertrude straight in the eye.

'What is your name?' bellowed Lady Wormtree.

'G-G-Gertrude,' she said.

'Detention,' shouted Lady Wormtree. 'Each week we are going to have a test. Get out your English books.'

The pupils didn't look happy at all. They didn't know what the test was going to be on, as they hadn't been given anything to learn.

'We are going to have a spelling test. I have chosen a topic that I know all children like – dinosaurs. So, let's get started. Spell Tyrannosaurus Rex.' This was followed by 'Triceratops'. All the children were terrified they would get them wrong. What a horrible start.

The next day everyone noticed how stupid Lady Wormtree looked. She wore a multi-coloured top, an enormous hat and white chinos.

'Today we are going to do some P.E.,' she said. Everyone was happy but they soon found out that it wasn't going to be fun at all.

'Girls, get out your tutus and give them to the boys,' she said. 'Boys, give your rugby kit to the girls.'

The boys were sad because they had to wear tutus and didn't want to dance ballet. The girls were sad because they didn't want to put on dirty rugby kits, all stiff with mud.

Lady Wormtree threw a rugby ball at the boys and said, 'You have a match against Armstrong High.' The boys were so embarrassed. How could they win looking like this? 'Girls, you have ballet grading in front of the whole school.'

Lady Wormtree was asking them to do such nasty things. Was she mad or did she secretly hate children?

Miss Horridhatcher's First Day
Charlotte Digney

The door opened and in stormed Miss Horridhatcher. All the children in the room shuddered as if a blast of cold air had swept over the classroom.

She walked with a tilting, side-to-side sensation. As she sat down she pulled out a piece of paper and said, 'I hope you know that we will be using paper for the register from now on, not the computer.'

The children looked sad. They loved their old teacher because she used to use the computer and she was a very nice lady.

'Ok,' she shouted, 'we begin. Lilken.'

'Miss, my name is not Lilken. It is – '

'Shut it, Lilken,' said Miss Horridhatcher.

The class took a deep breath.

There was one clever girl and her name was Mandy. Miss Horridhatcher called her Madrey, but I will call her Mandy.

'Now it's Maths,' said the teacher. 'We will start with the four times table. Six times four is twenty-six.'

'No,' said Mandy. 'Six times four is twenty-four.'

'Shut it, Madrey. Go to the head teacher.'

Mandy knocked on the office door.

A tall and slim woman appeared. 'What is it?' she asked.

'Hello, Mrs Feathersilk, I've been sent to see you by Miss Horridhatcher.'

'What have you done wrong?'

'I just said the four times table,' Mandy sobbed.

'No, no, do not cry. Tell me the story.'

So Mandy began to tell Mrs Feathersilk about the morning with Miss Horridhatcher.

On her way back to class, Mandy heard a scream and the sound of smashing glass. She dashed into the room and saw all the children leaning out of the broken window, looking at the ground.

Miss Horridhatcher was standing on top of her desk with both hands on her hips and a smug smile on her thin lips. Then there was a gigantic clatter as the desk gave way and the teacher fell. She lay on the floor with her legs and brown leather boots sticking in the air.

Just then, in burst Mrs Feathersilk. 'You are dismissed for throwing Max out of the window,' she said.

Mandy turned to Anthea. 'I wonder whose first day it will be tomorrow?'

Matilda Visits the National Gallery
Cameron Finnigan

'Right, twerps. I'm going to keep an eye on you so you'd better be nice,' said Miss Trunchbull. 'Look, a blue chicken!'

They walked into the gallery. 'Wow, it's amazing,' said Matilda.

The children were wondering how all the pictures fitted in the gallery.

'Right, hang your coats up through there and bring your lunchboxes over here,' commanded Miss Trunchbull. 'Ooh, I think I'm going to have a scrumptious lunch,' she said, taking five of the boxes for herself.

After lunch they had a look around at the pictures.

Sarah, the gallery guide, said, 'Just remember, don't get too close to them.'

There was a table next to some pictures. A boy called Bert put his foot out and Miss Trunchbull tripped over and hit the painting.

When Sarah came in she was so happy, but her face turned purple when she saw what Miss Trunchbull had done. 'JUST BECAUSE YOU'RE A TEACHER, DOESN'T MEAN YOU CAN TOUCH

THE PICTURES.'

'He tripped me up.' Miss Trunchbull turned to Bert. 'You are dead, worm!'

A person called Alex arrived to teach them history. All the questions he asked were answered by Matilda.

'She is a very clever girl, Miss Trunchbull,' said Alex.

'She's not clever. She's very stupid, actually.'

'Well I think she *is* clever.'

'You shouldn't be answering all those questions, stupid worm,' she said to Matilda. 'You're not clever.'

School Reports from Cruchem Hall
Maxim Hagan

Did you know that a frog is known as the jumping animal that jumps whenever it likes? Your son, William, is just like a frog jumping around like he needs the loo. Your son is a squirt, all slimy and slippery.

Did you know that a giraffe has the longest neck for a land animal? Unfortunately, your daughter Vanessa has been constantly licking her ears and bobbing her head up and down like a ball in water. She has to learn not to do this.

Cruncham Hall School Reports
Stuart Hearn

The giraffe is the tallest animal in the world. Your son Freddy cheats by stretching his long neck and looking at other people's work. When he is on his own he doesn't know any answers. He is so tall his head sticks out of the roof and he can't see his writing.

It is a curious truth that frogs always jump up and down. I think your son, Max, is related to a frog because he keeps on jumping up and down with the wrong answer!

Mr Hornetsting's First Day
Emma Hocking

The door opened and in stormed Mr Hornetsting. He peered around like a tiger.

'Good morning class,' he said.

'Good morning, Mr Hornetsting,' chirruped Form Three.

The teacher moved towards the desk like he was hunting his prey. He wore a green sleeveless shirt, spotted ankle-length socks, baggy grey trousers, a yellow checked tie and dark brown leather boots, not to forget a black pork-pie hat.

The class tried not to giggle. Suddenly they burst out laughing.

'Silence!' shouted Mr Hornetsting.

Form Three became deathly still.

'Right children, get your handwriting books out,' he bellowed.

'Sir,' said a small boy. 'I've forgotten my pencil.'

Mr Hornetsting turned purple with rage. He never thought anyone would come to *his* class without a pencil.

'You boy,' he raged, 'What is your name?'

'Bob King.'

'Come here,' shouted Mr Hornetsting. 'It's straight to the detention room for you. One hundred lines. I want you to write, "I will not lose my pencil".'

'But sir,' said Bob, 'I don't have a p – '

'Silence,' interrupted Mr Hornetsting. 'Off you go.'

The whole class started writing in their exercise books. No-one dared to breathe. Even the toughest boys were scared of the new teacher. Mr Hornetsting marched up and down the classroom, inspecting their work.

At last the bell rang.

'Playtime everyone,' said Mr Hornetsting, relieved he could get away from Form Three and have a relaxing cup of tea in the staff room.

Lord Bloodweed's First day
Rafee Jabarin

The door opened and in stormed Lord Bloodweed. When he moved, his chest puffed out like a robin. He wore a plaid, long-sleeved shirt, corduroy trousers, polka-dotted ankle socks and a pair of trainers. He had spiky black hair, was thin and sleek like a panther but had a face like a pig. Lord Bloodweed gave the class a cold glare.

Their first lesson was P.E. Once the children had changed into their kit they went to the hall. On the way Frank muttered to Max, 'I don't like this teacher,' but Lord Bloodweed was watching. 'DETENTION!' he shouted.

Frank shuddered. He would get in so much trouble with his mum.

In the hall a track was set out. When the children went round the track they got stuck on the monkey bars, were abandoned on top of the climbing frame and found they couldn't reach the basketball hoop.

'Come on, my grandmother can do better than that!' roared Lord Bloodweed.

The next lesson was science. They were making baking soda volcanoes.

'Now children, add five grams of baking soda to your volcano,' said the teacher.

Lily poured until the pointer was pointing at the five.

Lord Bloodweed glared at her. 'Hurry up Lily.'

Lily quickly poured in the other ingredients.

'Now stand back,' boomed Lord Bloodweed, as the volcanoes bubbled. All the volcanoes erupted slowly, but one burst out suddenly. It went up really high and splattered down on everyone.

'I said five grams, not five kilograms, you foolish child!'

Finally, after the worst day ever, it was time for the last lesson – art. The children watched nervously as Lord Bloodweed went around the art room handing out the equipment to paint with. As Adam poured some paint out of the bottle onto his palette, it stopped running, so he pressed harder and harder and even harder.

Let's just say it wasn't just Lord Bloodweed's socks that were polka-dotted.

Professor Icehammer's First Day
Kaillash Karthikeyan

The door opened and Professor Icehammer crept in. His footsteps were like hammers banging on the ground. He looked pale like ice and his eyes were the colour of frost. He wore blue trousers, pink ankle socks, a purple shirt and a green and yellow bowler hat. The class burst out laughing.

'Quiet, class,' said Professor Icehammer. 'Silence! Or you will get a pin through your hand!'

The class stopped laughing.

'Have you brought your English books? Stand up if you haven't,' roared Professor Icehammer.

Only two boys stood up. One of them said, 'My dog ate my book.'

'Stand outside the door!' said the teacher.

Instead they made chaos in the classroom.

'All of you pigs are not going to play!' said Professor Icehammer.

There was still chaos.

He left the room and locked the children in.

'Let us out!' they shouted.

'You'll stay there for the whole of break!'

Reports from Crunchem Hall School
Cecily Likeman

A water vole eats seventy per cent of its own body weight per day by chewing stalks. Your daughter Jane eats the same amount of pencils instead of doing her work.

Koalas eat eucalyptus leaves which make them go to sleep for up to twenty hours a day. It seems to me, judging by this year's work, that your son Nigel must have eucalyptus leaves for lunch.

The Chicken who wanted to Fly
Jack Lintern

Once there was a chicken who wanted to fly. His name was Gold. All the others teased him because he couldn't fly. One day he tried to make his own jet, but the wing fell off and he hurt himself. He was very sad. He was a very sad chicken.

The reason why Gold was so sad was because he really wanted to make a great escape out of the chicken run. This was because he imagined there must be much nicer places to live in the world.

He had another idea. He tried to make a catapult to fire him over the fence, but the strings snapped and he fell backwards and really hurt his head. Luckily he was OK, but needed another idea.

Later he said, 'Wait, I've got it,' but then he thought, 'Oh no, that won't work.'

He sat in his house all day feeling sad and trying to think of a way for his great escape. All the other chickens were outside playing with their friends, but Gold sat by himself with no-one to cheer him up.

He wished he had some friends to keep him company, but they were all laughing at him because he couldn't fly. He was very ashamed of himself and felt sad, tired and lonely. He knew there must be some nicer chickens out there waiting for him, but how was he going to escape to find them?

He calmed down so that his brain could whizz around for ideas. What was that? Yes he had it. He would make a wooden bike and ramp. He tried it, but the fence was just too high. What could he do to get out of this place!

Could he get a bigger chicken to help him fly over the fence? No, because none of them liked him. He was the saddest chicken in the world.

The others were all playing outside, laughing and eating again. They had bigger, comfier houses than Gold. It seemed as if the farmer liked them more than him. What should he do?

His next plan was to fly over the fence with a paraglider that the farmer had left out by accident. Luckily it was small enough for him to use, and YES IT WORKED!

Now it was time for an adventure. How long would it take him to find some nice chicken friends?

Mr Swordloo's First Day
Lottie Litherland

The door opened and in stormed Mr Swordloo with his chest puffed out like a robin. He wore a long sleeved shirt with checks, a solid-yellow cardigan, corduroy trousers, polka-dotted ankle socks and leather boots.

He sat on his desk and said, 'It's science. Go to the lab.'

One of the children was already there. He had a feeling the boy was up to something but he did not know what. The teacher sat down and saw spiders on his keyboard.

He jumped up and screamed, 'You, boy, in the cupboard!' He grabbed him by the ear, pushed him in and locked the door.

An hour later, he opened the door. 'What is your name, boy?' demanded Mr Swordloo.

'Jimmy Jam, Sir,' the boy said.

'Go to lunch, you worm, and take your spiders with you,' Mr Swordloo shouted, letting the boy out of the cupboard.

On the menu there was Worm Spaghetti with Ostrich Meatballs and for dessert Frogspawn Rice

Pudding served with Strawberry Jam. The whole school was queuing for lunch even though they didn't want it. Everyone was jealous of the vegetarians as they were given a lovely meal, like real pasta and vegetarian meatballs. For dessert they ate real rice pudding and raspberry jam.

After lunch it was Maths.

Mr Swordloo said, 'I want you to complete six maths pages in thirty minutes.' He tucked in his chair causing the loudest squeak. The class roared with laughter but then Mr Swordloo shouted, 'BE QUIET!'

Everybody stopped laughing apart from one pupil. 'You, boy. Get your toothbrush out of your school bag. Fetch Dribble, the Headmaster's dog, and groom him with it. Then I want you to brush *your* teeth.'

At the end of the day, Mr Swordloo went home to decide what punishments to give his class tomorrow.

**Class: 4M
Matilda**

Illustration by Amelie Rodriguez-Cobham

All the work in this section has been inspired by Roald Dahl's *Matilda*. The boys and girls have loved writing about terrifying teachers, pathetic parents, and crooked car salesmen. They also got their own back a bit by writing some school reports.

We hope that you will get as much pleasure from reading these pieces as we have got from writing them.

Illustration by Scarlett Newsam

The Superglue Eater
Luke Botterill

One day Matilda went up to her mum.

'Mum,' she said.

'Yes,' replied Mrs Wormwood.

'Make Dad stop selling cars dishonestly.'

'No!' screamed Mrs Wormwood.

'Why not?' asked Matilda.

'If you don't like how he gets money, don't eat what he spends his money on. No lunch for you,' shouted Mrs Wormwood.

'But –' muttered Matilda.

'No buts,' said Mrs Wormwood.

Matilda got angry and hungry, so she decided to get her own back.

The next day Matilda went to the library to think of a plan. Suddenly it came to her.

She rushed home, and on her way, she bought a tube of superglue. At home, she went into the bathroom and got her mum's toothpaste; she used a stool to reach, of course. She squirted all of the paste out and refilled the tube with superglue.

The next day Matilda was eating breakfast, when her mum came down and said, 'Mmmmmmm.'

'Speak up,' Mr Wormwood shouted.

'Mmmmm,' Mrs Wormwood choked.

'What did you say?' yelled Mr Wormwood.

'Mmmm,' she replied. Then she got a whiteboard and wrote on it, 'I can't open my mouth.'

'What game are you playing at?' exclaimed Mr Wormwood.

'I'm not playing a trick,' she wrote.

'Let me try,' Mr Wormwood offered, and he pulled hard on Mrs Wormwood's lips.

'Maybe Mum used superglue instead of toothpaste by mistake,' Matilda suggested.

'I know. I'll try scissors,' said Mr Wormwood. 'Matilda. Bed.'

All night Matilda could hear, 'Mmmmmmm.'

The next morning Matilda's mum marched into the kitchen with big, swollen lips and a few cuts.

'Don't say anything,' she babbled.

Nobody spoke to her all day because they were too scared.

As for Matilda, she read happily in her room for the rest of the day.

Theodore
Fabian Drew

Theodore's teacher, Miss Stapler, was the most strict woman on the planet and would never let anyone even breathe in her lessons. She kept everyone inside during playtime, lunch and even assembly, so at the end they would be bursting for air and energy. Theodore and the rest of his class couldn't stand it. She had super-dark hair and she was a giraffe compared to her desk. She looked like a stick, with arms and legs that could do times tables, write and make others do horrible things in unison. Her cardigan was covered in words like 'unison' and 'rules', but mostly it read 'discipline'. When one of the children answered a question wrong, she would hold his or her mouth open and drop a marble down their throat!

By the end of term, Theodore's stomach was full of marbles, and as soon as he got home he went over to the bin and coughed out all of the marbles he had swallowed during the day.

'I wish I hadn't got things wrong.' He coughed the last marble out of his stomach and went to do a super-long essay about metal. Revenge was swimming in his brain. Suddenly his mind turned up a brilliant plan.

Next day, Theodore explained to his friends how to set up a trap for Miss Stapler.

'Right. We need a desk, a pot, some marbles, a fan and a long piece of string,' he told them.

Oliver grabbed the pot of marbles and placed it on top of the fan that Olivia had put on the nearest table to the door. Theodore tied a piece of string to the fan's switch and tied the other end to a trip-wire. The trap was ready. Miss Stapler slammed the door open and stomped in. Unfortunately, she spotted the tripwire, but she pulled on it and set off the fan. The pot of marbles tipped over and smashed. Some of the marbles started gathering up in the wind, bumping into her.

Eventually, Miss Stapler's foot caught a field of them on the floor and she tumbled out of the classroom door. The whole class stared at the topsy-turvy Miss Stapler, rolling around like a kitten. She stumbled to her feet and zipped out of the building. She ran into her car and drove off, never to be seen again.

'Hurray!' screamed the class.

Matilda's Revenge
Tilly Lyons

Mrs Wormwood thought that Matilda needed a make-over, so one morning she told her, 'You are going to have a makeover.'

'Why? How?' Matilda asked.

'You will find out in a few minutes,' Mrs Wormwood snapped, and she locked Matilda up in a room.

It was quiet outside until someone was by the door, then in stomped Mrs Wormwood.

Matilda shouted, 'No!'

Matilda sat on the chair. Her mum put some lipstick on her and dyed her hair. When she was finished, she told Matilda to put on some dreadful clothes and shoes. The dress was bright pink and fluffy. The shoes - gosh – were so high, and don't mention them. Matilda did not like them.

Then her mum threw her in the car and drove off to Bingo. Matilda was feeling so embarrassed. She asked, 'Mummy? Please may I stay in the car?'

Mum replied, 'No, you earwig.'

They were at Bingo and everyone looked at Matilda in a state. Matilda just closed her eyes.

When the horrid Bingo was finally over, they went home and had dinner.

'I'm just going to the toilet,' Matilda said, but she actually went to the linen room. Then she got a big, white, fluffy bed sheet. Matilda took the sheet to her bedroom and cut out tiny little circles for the eyes. She put it over her body. She looked exactly like a ghost!

She walked into the kitchen and turned all the lights off. Then she made a sound like, 'Oooooh!'

Matilda's mother leapt up and spun round and screamed so loudly that the roof nearly came off! Mrs Wormwood slipped backwards over the coffee table and knocked the television over. The ghost ran off at the speed of light.

Mr Wormwood helped Mrs Wormwood up, as she was in shock.

Matilda definitely got her revenge.

For Sale – Ford Anglia Spectacular
Ophelia Mantell-Jacob

If you are looking for a reliable, comfortable and elegant car, that's really cheap to run, in fantastic condition and will make you the envy of your neighbours, then Mr Wormwood has the car for you.

A delicious sky-blue, A-reg Ford Anglia, environmentally friendly and a 100% bargain at only £50. This car has never *ever* gone wrong and is the cheapest car in the world to run.

It was previously owned by a little, old grandma of ninety-nine, so it's in fantastic condition. It's so comfortable that she could drive it between her living room and the shops without realising she had ever left the comfort of her sofa!

The fluffy, furry giraffe-skin seats are gorgeous and heavenly to sit on, and there are even extra covers (but the extras *do* cost money). Also available with this model are stripy, zebra-skin seat covers, and guess what? Exclusive, scrumptious polar bear-skin covers – a world first. The steering wheel is covered in sophisticated leopard-skin.

The car features a variety of cup holders of all shapes and sizes. There is also a new, sleek, 'sweet-treat', mouth-watering fridge in the boot, to keep your food cool on long journeys. It's worked by a cooler under the exhaust ... and don't forget the slide-back passenger seats that turn into beds!

Even better, it has headlights that come on *automatically* when it gets dark, and FREE WiFi and Satellite Navigation, plus fluffy, windscreen, polka-dot dice.

And that's not all: there's free candyfloss fuel. Don't worry if it runs out because there is always the extra big jar of volcanic, lime pickle stored in an enormous compartment by the fridge, to give the engine that extra boost of performance.

Better still, you won't believe it, but there are only 50 miles on the clock!

Mr Wormwood's cars always run smoothly and he is known the world over for his honesty and trustworthiness. He never sells a useless car.

Don't miss the Car of the Year Sale.

Don't walk past – come in.

Test drive and buy this luxury, irresistible, streamlined car.

But remember – no money, no car.

Mr Phlegmhair
Charlie McGuire

Our teacher was ill. The classroom door opened and in crashed Mr Phlegmhair! His wretched stench filled the classroom. Phlegmhair's hair wobbled exactly like a big mass of phlegm and his face was the same sickly colour. Mr PH's eyes were a horrid vine-green, his suit was a mean black and his snail-green boots were an insult to Simon Cowell.

'Sit down, you 'orrible excuse for human beings,' screeched Mr PH. I hesitated and sat down a fraction of a second after everyone else.

'Charlie McGuire, go and do fifty laps of the playground!'

The playground was as eerie as one of those graveyards you get in Scooby-Doo; all the trees were dead and there was no grass, just mud.

Suddenly my foot caught in something. I fell. Sharp rocks jutted out from all directions. I hit my head and everything went blank.

Some time later I came round and found myself in a huge, white room. People were moving about, making odd noises.

'Oobbly obbly gobble tack!'

I stared, amazed. They all looked like Mr PH.

I waited until they had gone, then sat up and ran towards what looked like a door. It opened. I climbed up a rocky wall then stood on the muddy ground of the playground.

'Tomorrow,' I thought, 'I'm going to find out what all this means.'

The next day Mr PH was meaner than ever. His hair wobbled triumphantly and his boots were the noisiest things next to a lion.

In Science, we were doing Space. Mr PH had just said, 'So there is a possibility that aliens live on Europa,' when it clicked. Mr PH was an alien! The white room was a spaceship and the people were Phlegm-haired aliens. Maybe they had tried to look human, but phlegm had got mixed in and that was why they had phlegm hair.

That evening I had an idea, and next day I took my water pistol to school, filled with Benadryl.

As soon as Mr Phlegmhair appeared, I squirted him. He dissolved into a puddle of slimy goo! We never saw him again and we got back our lovely, normal teacher.

Revenge for Noah
Noah Nejad

His name was Alex.

'No!' I shouted, when he broke my wooden fence that I had taken ages to build with my friend Tristan. I turned red with fury. I bellowed at him, 'You may have got me this time, but I will get you back.' I felt like punching him. I had to get revenge on him.

At school the next day and during break he went outside to meet his bullying gang. While he was outside with them, I went and got some slugs from the meadow and I put them in his pencil case.

After break, he rushed in and dug in his pencil case to get his pen. He thought he had found it. He pulled it out and looked at it.

'Aaaaaagh! It's a slug. I hate slugs,' screeched Alex.

The teacher told Alex to stop screaming or he would be in detention.

'Ha ha!' I said to myself, as the bell rang for lunch, and I hurried to get there before Alex could bully me.

At lunch break I went out, but I didn't realise that Alex had set up an ambush. I walked out and he grabbed me by the shirt.

'Aaaagh!' I screamed. 'Please don't hurt me,' but he did. He kicked me and he hit and punched me. I had to pay him back.

In Games, I said to him, 'Alex, you're a bully.'

Alex turned red with fury. He looked like a bull that was about to charge. He grabbed me by the hair and his spiky boot was in the air and on its way to kicking me, when Mr Corp looked my way.

'Alex. Don't you dare kick him. Detention for you!' Mr Corp bellowed.

Alex never bullied me again.

Miss Snailsnot
Max Newark

The door opened, and in stomped Miss Snailsnot. She howled, 'Good morning, stupid class,' with an evil glare. 'We are going to be doing Maths, today.'

All the children saw all her warts and they absolutely smelled. Her snot was dangling like a bungee jump. Her hair was like a crows' nest just being built. She looked like she ate flies for breakfast, lunch and dinner.

'SIT DOWN, YOU EVIL LOT! Now work, you minions.'

The children groaned.

'But you haven't told us what problem to solve?'

Miss Snailsnot stormed over to Tim's desk. She picked him up and whacked him with her cane.

'OOOUUUCH!'

But Tim had found a pin on the ground and an elastic band. He pulled back the pin with the elastic band and let go. It zoomed through the air and hit her in the eye.

'Who did that?'

The class fell silent. She stormed around the class, glaring at everyone in turn.

They remained silent. Then the bell went *RING*.

Everyone rushed out of the room like Usain Bolt.

Miss Snailsnot narrowed her eyes. 'I will find you again, one day. MUHAHAHA!'

The children had had a very lucky escape.

Mr Flywax
Scarlett Newsam

The door opened and in stomped Mr Flywax. Mr Flywax wore tufted jeans, muddy brown shoes with untied shoe laces and a very stinky, snotty rugby shirt that hadn't been washed in ages. He clutched two canes with extremely sharp bits on the end. He had the largest beard you could ever imagine. He had hairy ears and a black belt.

'SIT DOWN RIGHT NOW!' boomed Mr Flywax. 'I will take the register,' he sneered. 'Maia Pest?'

'It's Maia *West*, Sir,' said Maia.

'I DON'T CARE!' screeched Mr Flywax. 'Max Sewer?' said Mr Flywax.

'It's Max *Newark*, Sir,' said Max.

After fifteen more names had been called out and all had mistakes in them, Mr Flywax finally announced, 'No lunch for you lot!'

'Why?' asked George. 'I'm really hungry.'

'Because I say so,' bellowed Mr Flywax.

'Well,' said Mr Flywax, 'time for *my* lunch,' and he took a packet of extra spicy beef crisps from his pocket.

'Awwww,' said Vish.

'It's not fair!' screamed Sheev.

'Shut up, Fish and Scream, and just sit down. NOW!' said Mr Flywax.

'I need the loo,' said a few people at the back of the classroom.

'You'll have to wait until you get home,' said Mr Flywax.

In the afternoon, Mr Flywax exclaimed, 'Afternoon register. Scarlett Nuisance?' he said.

'Yes, Sir,' said Scarlett.

At that moment, Mr Candy opened the door. 'I just wanted to check how you were doing,' he said.

'HE'S TORTURING US!' screamed Ben.

'SHUT UP, PHLEGM!' bellowed Mr Flywax.

'I'll take him away, shall I, children?' said Mr Candy.

'YESSSS!' screamed the children, and Mr Candy swung Mr Flywax over his shoulder.

'I'll be back,' menaced Mr Flywax.

The door slammed. Everything was silent.

Rotten Riot
Gil Nowak

Riot was a mean, keen killing machine. His fist was like a stone, fifteen metres thick. His legs were so fat that if you put a pin in, they would explode.

Once he punched me and I fell over backwards. I really wanted to get revenge, and I had just the thing to stop him from doing it again. I had been planning this for years, and now I was going to act it out. The plan was to ambush him with water guns.

The next day, when he walked past my door, BANG! He was soaked. Then I saw him change direction. Riot faced *my* door. His fist punched through it and he raced in.

'Get out, you overgrown sausage,' I shouted.

Riot did not listen to me. He picked me up and pulled my hair.

'Stop it, stop it!' I screamed. I kicked out, but my feet bounced off Riot's fat legs. He threw me on the ground and stomped out.

'That's it,' I thought. 'Enough of being bullied.' My revenge had failed.

'I must do better next time,' I said to myself.

Then I had a great idea. On the next street lived

another big bully called Gruff; he was like a mountain.

So, next morning, I hid behind the wall as Gruff came stomping up the road. Riot was coming up the road behind him. I jumped up and threw a rotten egg. It landed on Gruff's head. Gruff turned around in horror, and saw Riot behind him.

I hid behind the wall.

Riot looked at Gruff and wondered why he was covered in smelly egg.

'You are going to be really sorry,' yelled Gruff.

'What do you mean?' said Riot.

'Look at my head, you nitwit,' shouted Gruff, and he chased Riot all around the town.

Now Riot is too scared to come out of his house.

Now he knows how I felt. The best revenge ever.

Washing Up Liquid Revenge!
Joseph Reece

One morning Mr Wormwood boomed at Matilda, 'Go to Bingo with your mother!'

'What a good idea,' Mrs Wormwood smiled.

This made Matilda blush scarlet red. She hated Bingo and she would do anything not to go. She tiptoed upstairs avoiding Mr Wormwood, and muttered, 'I'm NOT going to Bingo,' and she stamped her feet not knowing what to do.

Then she had an idea. 'I'm going to put rats in her larder.' But Matilda didn't have any rats. 'I know,' she thought, 'I'm going to pierce a hole in Mum's pillow, take out the feathers and fill it up with washing-up liquid, like my dad puts sawdust in the engines of the cars he sells!'

Matilda dragged her feet into the car to go to Bingo, but she was excited about her plot to get revenge.

That evening, when everyone was asleep, she crept downstairs and used her mum's best tongs to grab the feathers out of the pillow. Then she got the green washing-up liquid and squirted all of it into the pillow. The pillow felt squidgy and squashy.

'It's a battle of wits,' she thought.

The next day, at bed time, Matilda swapped the pillow. She put the nice pillow in her room and the squidgy and squashy one in Mrs Wormwood's bed.

Matilda was lying in her bed, gazing at the stars, waiting, when she heard a horrendous scream. It was coming from Mrs Wormwood's bedroom.

Matilda hadn't had the most perfect day, but she had a clean revenge and she went to sleep peacefully.

For Sale
Amelie Rodriguez-Cobham

For Sale; a gorgeous Discovery 4. An irresistible scarlet-red, it has soft, elegant seats with heating. It has a sleek, snow-leopard steering wheel and a 2 metre boot, made by professional craftsmen and engineers. This scrumptious, top-of-the-range Land Rover has a fridge for keeping the champagne cool on a glorious summer's day. It has a shiny, spare wheel, unbreakable, smoked-glass windows and a top speed of 780mph. It is guaranteed for a month before it needs refilling!

This car has the ability of a mountain goat when off the beaten track, yet it assumes the poise and agility of a gazelle on the motorway.

It was owned by one sensible lady, who only used it once a month at just 20mph, for shopping.

Free satnav included.

Yours for only £4,000.

Andrew Jones
Tristan Rouviere-Hyde

Andrew Jones is my dad and he is as mean as a blood-sucking bat. He is tall and thin and really unfair. He is very bossy. He loves to suck on black pudding. He doesn't speak; he roars, as loud as a lion.

One day he tore up my painting.

'What a mess! There's no point in taking *that* to school. It's rubbish!' he roared.

'No! Don't do that,' I shouted. 'It's my homework.'

'Too late. You'll have to do it again.'

'But Dad, we don't have any paper left!'

I turned and went to get ready for school. I felt sad and useless because I had worked hard on it. I was worried that I might get a detention from my teacher. I felt angrier with every step I took forward.

The following day was Saturday. My dad had to go to work and he made me go with him. This was the time for me to get him back!

When he had to go out to the garage, I found a bundle of rope and balanced it on the top of the office door.

When he came back in, he opened the door. The

rope fell down and it coiled up around him. He was stuck in it like a fly in a spider's web. He was shouting for help to escape from the rope. He shouted so much that he lost his voice. He couldn't shout any more.

When the cleaners arrived, they found him struggling and tangled up in the rope. It took two men to untie him.

That was the day my dad found out that shouting doesn't help. And he learned to be patient.

For Sale
Vish Senthil Kumar

Luxury BMW sports car for sale. Its steering wheel is made of soft tiger-skin, which shines like diamonds. The seats are covered in gorgeous lion-skin. The windscreen wipers are made of sharp, metal blades which take every single drop of water off the screen.

This super car was once owned by the Lord Mayor of London and is painted in gold paint, which sparkles in the sun. The windows have been professionally tinted a dark blue and the car comes with a free satnav with all the roads you will ever need. Try it out and see the difference.

This car is very rare and exclusive; you can't resist its scent. The boot size is big enough to fit ten suitcases. The top speed is 150mph and it runs swiftly on a smooth road, making you feel epic.

This car is guaranteed for a whole week and only costs £2000. Buy it, and all your friends will be jealous.

Payback Time for Mr Snakespit
Luke Smith

Mr Snakespit is the most evil and ugliest person in the universe. He gives out so many detentions; I estimate about one million! He once went to someone's birthday party and blew out all his candles! But don't get me started on that story.

One day, my best friend Luke and I bumped into him by accident. He shoved Luke off the upper corridor and 'SPLAT!' He had to go to hospital and was there for the rest of the term.

That drew the line. I was going to get my own back on Mr Snakespit, whether he was my teacher or not.

That night I decided on my plan. I would go to school early and place pins on his chair, which I would carefully paint the same colour as the chair. Then I would hang a net above the same chair, attached to a rope and a pull-cord, so when he sat on the pins he'd jump up and into the net. At the same time I would pull the rope, trapping him for the rest of the day!

The next morning I got up early as planned. I grabbed my jacket and popped on my socks and shoes. I realised I might need someone else to help, so on the way to school, I stopped by at Joe's house and told him my plan. He said it was foolproof.

We ran to school and set up my trap. I placed the pins messily on the chair and Joe used some super-strong glue to fix the ropes to the ceiling and he fixed the net to them. I tied a long piece of string to the ropes and Joe ran it under the chairs, all the way to my place.

I heard Mr Snakespit stomping along the corridor.

'Quick. He's coming. Back to your seat.'

We dashed to our seats.

He stomped in and jumped onto the chair.

'YEEOOWWW!' he screeched and went shooting up like a rocket, and into the net. I tugged the string for all I was worth and he was trapped.

I smiled evilly. Everyone cheered and then we stampeded outside to play, leaving him struggling inside the net!

When we came back in, there was a hole in the window and he had gone. We never saw Mr Snakespit again.

Mr Bullsnot
Jacob Spooner

The door opened and in charged Mr Bullsnot. He was huge. He had fire-smoke pouring out of his nostrils and his voice was so loud it would beat a jet engine. He had muscles so big he could lift a million trucks weighing two million tonnes at once.

'Shut up and sit down!' roared Mr Bullsnot.

I was horrified by the sight of him. He was smelly and thin, with a pointy nose and sticky-out teeth.

At lunchtime the look on my face must have shown what I was thinking, as he came over and threw me out of the room.

As I sat on my own in the playground, watching through the window that I had left by, I decided that I would get my revenge later that day.

The afternoon passed without much damage. Mr Bullsnot snorted, shouted, breathed fire and exploded with rage at least twenty times. Doublehead, my very clever best friend, and I tried to hide at the back of the classroom, passing notes and sweets, and filling our time by flicking balls of paper at Mr Bullsnot.

It was later that day that I carried out my revenge.

I put golden syrup on Mr Bullsnot's chair. The whole class roared with laughter as he stood up and the chair came with him. Part one complete.

Part two of my plan was to place a whoopee cushion on his chair. He sat down and 'Whooomph!!' went the whoopee cushion.

I can only say that I was rather pleased with myself.

Mr Fatdevil
Sheev Tirbhowan

The door smashed open. Rolling like a boulder came Mr Fatdevil, a bottle of coke in his right hand and a bloody sausage in his left. He looked a state! His patched shirt was ripped and he was wearing no tie at all. He had crazy hair and black teeth.

The first thing he yelled was, 'Sit down, you stupid children!' He stomped to his desk and screamed, 'Get on with your work.'

'What work?' Bob asked.

'Shut up,' Mr Fatdevil roared. 'It's Maths.'

Bob blubbed, 'I don't like Maths.'

Mr Fatdevil growled, 'Well, tough,' and he threw the book in poor Bob's face. Bob was crying.

At last, the bell rang for playtime.

'Get out, horrible, slimy children, or I'll eat you up!' Mr Fatdevil yelled, and the children shot out of the classroom.

Mr Fatdevil went to his tea-break and he stuffed his face with chocolate biscuits, cakes, scones, ice cream and marshmallows. His face was covered in crumbs and looked as spotty as leopards' fur.

After break, it's P.E.,' Mr Fatdevil roared. 'So get

your bags and let's go.'

At Bathampton, Mr Fatdevil was teaching the boys and he chose to demonstrate how to tackle on Bob.

'Oh no. Are you going mad?' Bob wobbled, as Mr Fatdevil tackled him. His stomach hit Bob's face and Bob went flying over the trees, over the houses, over the town and over the hills.

Bob's friend, Ben, was so angry that he grabbed the rugby ball and lobbed it as hard as he could possibly throw it, straight at Mr Fatdevil's giant, peachy stomach.

Mr Fatdevil exploded like fireworks and everybody cheered.

Mrs Muffin and the Secret Portal
Ben von Arx

The door opened and in blew the wind. It was very strong. It was pulling me in and I was sucked into the classroom.

Mrs Muffin was the loveliest teacher, with her hair shining brightly like diamonds in the sky. She held the most magnificent book the children had ever seen. She wore shoes that shone so brightly that the children thought they were smiling at them. She was carrying a big bunch of clinking and clanking keys. What would they open? But the best thing of all was the glorious book she was clutching as she entered the classroom.

'That looks like a good book, Mrs Muffin,' said Matt. 'Can you read to us?'

Mrs Muffin explained to the children that *she* had never read the book because it was locked and she did not know how to get it open.

'Why don't you try opening the book with the keys?' asked Matt.

'Will you help me to figure out the key order to unlock it?'

The children were all very excited and cried out,

'Yes, we will help you crack the code.'

They looked at the keyholes very carefully. They looked at the keys as well. Which one would fit in?

They managed to figure out the first two keys, but then the last one was tricky because they did not know which one to put in. They tried all the different options and finally, the book opened.

Inside the book was a message. The message was: LOOK BEHIND THE MAP ON THE WALL AND YOU WILL UNCOVER A SECRET.

The children rushed to the wall and carefully removed the map, which was pinned to it. And there it was. A secret portal! Nobody knew where this would lead to.

'Let's jump inside and find out,' yelled Gomez.

They all jumped in, one after another, like a roller-coaster ride. They landed up on Mrs Muffin's kitchen floor!

'Well, since we're here, let's have cookies and milk!' said Mrs Muffin.

The children were all very pleased that they had helped work out how to open the book.

Makeover Mayhem
Maia West

I always dread the sweltering hot afternoons when my mum comes back from work for Bingo. This particular Tuesday I was going to hate it more than ever though. Mum swaggered in, revealing her bulging legs. As she flicked back her mop of silver-dyed, flowing hair, she flashed one of her smug film-star grins at Dad, nearly splitting her face in two. Then she grabbed my hair and dragged me into her dressing room.

'MUM, what are you doing?' I screamed.

Several strands of my hair drifted to the floor.

'Be quiet!' Dad exploded.

We emerged into the butter-yellow dressing room, which was crammed with deadly make-up instruments. Mum threw me into a chair and gazed at her reflection in the mirror.

'Oh, aren't I beautiful?!' she said mistily.

She started curling her hair into tight ringlets. Her head looking like a plate of spaghetti in hair curlers! She started putting on oodles of fake tan, smearing bright blue make-up all over her eyelids and donning a heavy layer of mascara on her eyelashes. She was bright orange, looking like an oversized gorilla!

'Now it's your turn!' Mum loomed over me and I shrank back.

'NOOOOO!' I shouted.

This was too much. She was braiding my hair into tiny, little plaits, with pink bows on the bottom and purple beads. With shocking pink blusher on my cheeks and a magenta, frilly frock, I looked a complete girly dumbnut. It was time for revenge.

Early next morning, I took my dad's purple hair tonic and went into the washing room. My mum's cream, lace dress was in the laundry basket waiting to be washed. I stuffed it into the washing machine with some powder and half the bottle of blacky-purple hair tonic. Ha!

After breakfast, Mum swaggered into the washing room to retrieve her favourite dress. Seconds later there was a deafening scream, and she stormed in clutching a blacky-purply bundle of ripped up cloth.

'What happened to my dress?' she screeched. 'I think this has something to do with you or your wretched father and his stupid hair tonic.'

'He must have left it in his pocket,' I said, innocently, and Mum stormed off. And that was that!

Mr Beetlebum
George White

The door opened and in strode a dark figure. It was Mr Beetlebum! He was a terrible sight. He wore black sunglasses to hide his red, bloodshot eyes. His face was like a big tomato and his teeth were so blackened with decay they were the colour of coal. His hair was short and straight, like a buffalo. His stainless steel dagger was as sharp as the spike on the Eiffel Tower. He wore ragged, Fatface trousers and top. His trousers bulged because of his beetle-like bum. His hobnail boots were as sharp as iron thorns and they looked like they wanted to kick you.

He roared, 'Sit down and shut your cake 'oles!'

We all knew he was nothing like Mrs Warmpie. She sat in class giving out house points.

Our first lesson was History. We were learning about the First World War. Mr Beetlebum got out a box. He told us to look inside.

There were about twenty-five war rifles in it. We stepped back. Mr Beetlebum took one out.

He said, 'If one of you talks, I'll shoot ya!'

Three lessons later the cutest girl in the class, Rhianna, started chatting to Bob. Mr Beetlebum noticed. He stalked up to her and shouted, 'No talking in my class!' Then, quick as a flash, he picked Rhianna up and chucked her out of the open window!

The next lesson was Science. I just had to survive this class, then Mrs Warmpie would be back.

We went outside with the parachute men we had made in DT a few days ago. All twenty of us trudged up the steep hill to the astroturf, with twenty bottles, all loaded with baking soda and vinegar.

Mr Beetlebum walked over to the biggest bottle.

'I'm going to show you how to make these puny, little toys fly,' he yelled. 'You put the lid of the bottle on and – '

'WHOOSH!' The bottle went up, with Mr Beetlebum still holding on. The bottle soared higher and higher, until it flew out of sight.

Full of excitement we sent our bottles up and the parachute men floated down.

We never saw Mr Beetlebum again.

Miss Perfumebomb
Daniel Wigfield

The door opened and in trotted Miss Perfumebomb.

'Good morning, class,' she screeched, happily.

'Good morning, Miss Perfumebomb,' chanted 3P.

Miss Perfumebomb looked lovely. She had strawberry perfume and the class could always smell the nice scent. She wore the same clothes every day; not the same actual clothes, for she had lots of clothes that were exactly the same. Her top was always stripy pink and purple, so you can probably see that her favourite colours were pink and purple, but actually she also liked red. She had red lipstick, red nail varnish and red, glossy, shiny shoes, like rubies. She had beautiful, white diamond earrings that glittered in the sunlight. Miss Perfumebomb had sharp, bright blue eyes with very long eyelashes. Her hair was long, shiny and flaming, like the sun and stars.

After morning register Miss Perfumebomb went to the staffroom to mark some Humanities, and Mr Ratslug banged into the classroom for Maths.

'Good morning, you sluggish lot,' he boomed. 'You there, Ronald. Clear up the slimy mess you made,' and he pointed to the trail of slime coming from under the door.

'But, Sir, you made this mess,' said Ronald.

'Don't answer back. You'll be cleaning up the whole school as a punishment,' Mr Ratslug boomed.

Mr Candy, the headmaster, was in his office next door and he heard the kerfuffle.

'What is this slime on the floor? And did I hear someone say a pupil had to clean up the whole school?' Mr Candy asked. 'Mr Ratslug. I won't have this silly nonsense about children cleaning up the school. Come to my office. We need to have a chat. Just wait quietly for a minute or two, 3P, and Miss Perfumebomb will come to teach you Maths instead.'

'Yaaay!' screamed 3P, in relief.

It was lovely to have Miss Perfumebomb back, and later that day Mr Marshmallow, the fat caretaker, was seen dragging Mr Ratslug out of the building. The school never saw him again.

School reports
Ophelia Mantell-Jacob

Did you know that a sheep can only concentrate for ten seconds? I wonder if your son Phillip is somehow related to a sheep?

Maia West

The frog is a strange creature, which bounces up and down nearly all the time. Ever since Andy arrived at this school he has displayed this strange and special talent. From my desk I can just see him, bobbing up and down on his toes with his hand directly up, waiting for the rare moment when I will let him proudly tell me the wrong answer!

George White

When a wolf howls it can be heard over four miles away. Ethan talks as if *I* am four miles away!

Matilda Limerick
Scarlett Newsam

There once was a child with a book,

Whose parents were actually crooks.

Her parents would shout,

'Kick that silly child out!'

But she just kept on reading that book.

A Little White Cat
Tilly Lyons

There once was a little white cat,

Who liked to curl up in a hat.

She loved too much dinner,

Was no longer thinner,

So the cat had to sleep on a mat.

The Snail in 4M
Ben von Arx

There once was a snail in 4M,

Who was slow at his work with a pen.

The teacher would shout

When he was about,

'Stop slouching and do it again!'

Year 5. Mrs Hardware's Set

As part of our work on *The Chronicles of Narnia*, we have been exploring the fantasy genre of *The Lion, the Witch and the Wardrobe* and creating our very own fantasy worlds.

We have been focusing on the use of the senses to highlight our ideas; using tangible feelings and emotions that can be seen, heard, touched, smelled or felt.

Illustration by Tanya Ahmed

Illustration of Upside Down Land by Joshua Moir

Sweet Land
Tanya Ahmed

As I stepped into the wardrobe I brushed past a dress that felt soft like bubblegum. I stuck my tongue out and licked the dress; it tasted of strawberry.

'Wow, what amazing yummy clothes,' I thought.

I could smell peppermint on the shirts; they had peppermint buttons. There was a skirt made of cola bubblegum, which had strawberry lace frills. I tried it on and it fitted perfectly.

There were beautiful clothes made out of all sorts of sweets. I heard drops of chocolate hitting the warm floor and melting. I walked on and found another line of clothes.

'This must be an enormous wardrobe,' I thought. I saw clothes of different sizes and wondered who had made them all. I kept on shuffling in, deeper and deeper. I felt a cold wind hitting my spine, making me shiver.

Then I realised there is no wind in a wardrobe. I turned and saw a river of chocolate. I looked around some more. There was a tree made out of jelly with gummy bears dangling from its branches and lollipops with swirls of different colours dotted around the land. Ice cream was dripping on top of some strawberry laces. I walked over the red laces and they tickled my feet. I saw a bridge made out of jelly, so I leapt on it. I jumped up and down cautiously so I didn't fall into the chocolate river. I kept on walking until I saw a small red figure walking slowly towards me. Gradually, the person became clearer and I saw it was a gummy bear. I screamed, and so did the sweet.

'A talking gummy bear,' I said.

'A talking human,' said the gummy bear.

'Hello, nice to meet you,' I said.

'Hello,' he replied. 'How did you get here?'

'Well, I went into a really large wardrobe and at the back I saw this place. It suddenly started raining chocolate!'

'Quick, go back, the river is flooding!' said the gummy bear.

I dived into the wardrobe and the land disappeared.

Sweet Land
Tom Bertinet

As I step into the large wardrobe, I push aside old cooks' hats and aprons. I walk further in expecting to feel the hard wood of the wardrobe, but to my surprise I feel soft grass. I bend down to pick a green blade. It tastes like apple liquorice.

I carry on exploring this magical world and I smell caramel. In the distance I can just see a caramel waterfall plummeting to the ground. I take a few steps towards the waterfall to investigate, but collide with a large, white pole. I look up and see it's a giant lollipop tree with red and green colours in the shape of a Catherine Wheel. It smells of strawberry and lime.

I carry on walking, and more and more colourful lollipop trees appear in front of my eyes. On the hillside I see gummy bears playing around a gingerbread house. I sprint towards the house in excitement, but have to stop as an edible car, with a marshmallow man inside it, comes humming down a lane that seems to be made of Maltesers. I look up again and see pink clouds.

'I guess they are made of candyfloss,' I say to

myself.

I carry on with my exciting journey and suddenly I bump into a red gummy bear. 'Aaagggrrrhhhh!' I scream.

We both run away. I hide behind a lollipop tree. Then we slowly step towards each other.

'Good day! Jolly good day!' says the bear. 'I am Gary. Gary the gummy bear.'

'Well, glad to meet you, Gary,' I say.

'I hope you don't mind me asking,' says Gary, 'but who are you? You're not blue or red or purple like the other gummy bears. Where are you from?'

'I am Tom Bertinet from the United Kingdom. I am a human not a gummy bear.'

'Cool!' says Gary. 'Would you like to see the rest of Sweet Land?'

Sweet Land
Daisy Collett

As I step through the wardrobe I feel soft candyfloss. There's a bright light ahead and I take a few steps further in. I push the candyfloss out of the way and see a wonderful place! 'This can't be right,' I think.

I see gummy bears laughing and playing, and a gingerbread man slurping some cherryade. I taste the sweetness of the melted ice cream on the hills. I hear a sherbet snake slithering on the ground and see some baby gummy people jumping on the jelly path and a few little gummy bears as well.

A toffee apple tree is just in front of me and a strawberry person is relaxing in a pool of cola. Some warm chocolate drips from the top of the wardrobe onto me.

I think to myself, 'I must get back to the house to tell the others about this place.'

But then a cheeky jellybaby takes me into a candy and chocolate house. After I have seen the house I carry on exploring the whole land.

A gummy bear says to me, 'Hiya, if we follow the jelly path we can go to my house.'

'Ok,' I say.

As we jump along the jelly path, I see a cantering fudge horse.

The gummy bear says, 'I'm so sorry to be rude. My name is Chew-ems. What's your name?'

'Oh,' I say, 'My name is Daisy.'

We carry on jumping until we get to the end of the path.

'Here we are, this is my house,' Chew-ems announces.

As I step into the house, the first thing I see is a bright room covered in sweets and chocolates. I hear a clink.

'What was that, Chew-ems?' I ask, as he sits me and himself down.

'Look, there is a very sour queen and she has my gummy babies and has forced me to kidnap you. But I feel horrid, so run as fast as you can to get away because she knows you are here.'

'Thanks for having me,' I say, and off I run!

The Wilderlands
Chris Donovan

I stumbled through the wardrobe and a blast of cold wind lashed my face.

How can wind come from the back of a wardrobe? Perhaps it's a secret passage.

I charged onwards and tripped. I felt something bristly on my skin. It smelled like grass. I stood up and saw an immense valley with a green forest and a bubbling swamp at its base. Snowy mountains looked down on it. I tasted the air: peace, nature and a flicker of malice.

Suddenly I heard a colossal booming noise – THWOOD, THWOOD, THWOOD! I turned around. A massive shadow loomed over the mountain: the shadow of a dragon. I looked up and stumbled backwards. A fiery red dragon thundered over the top of me. Its celestial, red scales glistened in the shimmering sunlight and as the dragon flew off I heard a guttural, bellowing roar.

Some bizarre creature scuttled down towards the woods making a squeaking noise. It had swamp-green, leathery skin and the general looks of a frog, except for cat-like whiskers and large ears.

Instinctively, I followed it.

The odd-looking frog led me to the forest. I chased it along a narrow path. As I ran, I glimpsed savage bite marks on the trees. Then my foot caught on something. A thin rope snatched me round the ankles, my legs were whipped out from underneath me and I was swung upside down. The weird frog stood beneath me. A large goblin, clad in crude grey armour with a cruel, jagged sword at his side, appeared.

'Who are you?' I asked. 'Please let me down.'

'My name – Grobsnatch. I goblin, Bark Biter clan I am. I guard. Toad Squeal here, lead you to us.' He pointed to the creature standing next to him.

The goblin narrowed his eyes and observed me.

'If you make fire we keep you. But if you don't – '

He put his finger to his throat and drew a line across it.

Sweet Land
Olivia Fee

I open the wardrobe and step inside. I feel bags full of sweets brush against my arms and at the end of the wardrobe I see some trees. But the weirdest thing is they don't have leaves; they are made of candyfloss and have candy canes hanging on them. I lift my head and open my mouth and a tonne of sherbet falls onto my tongue. It's sooo sour.

'This isn't right!' I say, quite loudly.

I hear a fudge horse trotting along a Daim bar road. There's the smell of the most delicious Thorntons chocolate. I can see giant cola bottles and a little gummy bear. A group of jelly girls are jumping over a strawberry-lace skipping rope on some candy grass. I'm standing on a path made of chewing gum and there are some mints along the edge. I hear some flying gummy bears that sound a bit like badgers snuffling for food.

'That's odd!' I say.

A bubblegum boy comes up to me and says in a squeaky voice, 'What are you?'

'I'm a girl if you didn't realise,' I reply.

'Me and my friends will get you a deckchair and

some shades as you are so nice,' he says.

'I'll help you, if you want.'

I walk over to where the boys are standing. I put on the sunglasses and help the boys carry the deckchair across to the spot I had been standing on. I sit on the chair and the boys run away into a gingerbread house. It's only now that I realise that Sweet Land is scorching hot, like an oven!

A clean, white tray appears on my lap. On it there's a bowl of mint choc-chip, strawberry, chocolate and vanilla ice cream all mixed together. Yum! There are also two, freezing cold drinks. One is Seven Up and the other is Coke. I drink them both in super-quick time. The ice cream tastes so delicious. I can see a girl with the same tray as me, eating it. It's totally sugar.

The World of Dragons
Christopher Godwin

My Narnia is a dragon land. As I stepped through the wardrobe I felt the scaly surface of dragon-skin coats brush against my shirt and saw the bright light of flaming eggs lighting the way.

Three more steps and I got dazzled by the swarming mass of screeching dragons. One more pace and I tripped over a small dragon known as the toxic-cockroach-dragon. I backed away quickly and smelled the unpleasant pong of a stink-dragon. I then tasted the sweet juice of a huge water-dragon tree and looked up. A huge flame-blast dragon was swooping down on a small nightshade. Then a streak of yellow light darted past me and landed in a nearby tree. It was a large spark-dragon, the fastest of the dragons, I assumed.

A swarm of what looked like bees gathered around a mimic-dragon, which turned the colour of the tree it was sitting on to try to disguise itself from the attackers. (Had it had stolen their honey?) Suddenly a flame erupted out of nowhere and an average-sized glass-dragon swooped down to land on a flame tree. As soon as that happened, a baby fire-balling dragon fell out and landed on a fully-grown water spout, which immediately put out its flames. I ran to rescue the fire-balling dragon and chucked it back in a tree. The wrong one, a wood tree not a flame tree, so the leaves set on fire and the little dragon fell out again. He started to walk towards me. I turned and came face to face with the toxic-cockroach-dragon. I tripped over, but luckily the fire-balling dragon set the mad cockroach alight before it reached me.

I decided to call him Flash and we became friends. We stuck together.

Next day we were playing Hide-and-Seek, when I found his scaly tail poking out of the wardrobe. I followed him inside, tripping over one of the coats. I was reaching out to grab him, when we both tumbled out of the wardrobe and back into my house.

I had my very own pet dragon in my house. Life was going to be a lot of fun!

Gaming Land
Theo Laver

As I step through the old, dusty, crumbly wardrobe I feel warm and cosy among the designer, fur coats and the showers of moth balls. Reaching the back of this immense space, I spy a DVD lying on the floor next to some fantastically expensive speakers. I pick up the disc. The warmth of my hand transfers to it and I begin to hear music and see flashing lights like laser beams darting in front of me. I close my eyes and amazingly it's if I've become a human DVD player.

Instead of the blackness of my eyelids, I see a world inhabited by characters from every game on the planet. The music is getting louder, but it is chaotic, like the sound of a hundred stereos all tuned to different radio stations. I put my hands to my head, clutching hard to shield myself from the din. As I raise my hands I drop the DVD. The noise subsides.

I open my eyes. Where am I?

I can see endless reams of doors marked with well-known game names. The floor of this space is plain, dazzling white. There are houses for characters built with old bricks, and triangular windows made from PlayStation4 controllers. It smells of burning discs and new plastic. I feel warm and cosy here as it's full of familiar characters. Suddenly an extremely tiny policeman from a robbing game comes up to me.

"Ello, 'ello, 'ello, what ya' doin' here old chap?' he says as he looks up at me.

'Excuse me sir, but I'm not from here. I have come from the wardrobe.' I wasn't really sure how you should speak to a real-life gaming character, especially one with a tazer!

'Interesting - hmmm. Well don't get up to mischief or you'll never come back.' He pointed towards the gaming cell and I shuddered.

I walked on, taking in all the bizarre sights.

I will spend one night here and one night only!

Dancing Land
Lollie McKenzie

As I stepped into the wardrobe I felt the scratch of stiff netting and the smooth slither of silk costumes hanging up. Walking further in, I trod on a sparkly, new, high-heeled shoe.

'What strange things to put in an old wardrobe,' I thought.

I could smell something, a bit like perfect coconut milk and the sweet tang of fresh mango. There was a light ahead, not a few inches away where the back of the wardrobe ought to have been, but a long way off.

I followed it and saw several girls twirling around, and about thirty ladies performing a dance that looked like it was second nature to them. With their beautiful, pink leotards and tutus, they looked like pink flamingos flying over a serene lake. Behind them, a band played exquisite music.

I was standing in a world of happiness, a world of dancing.

Illustration by Lollie McKenzie

Wrinkle Land
Ben McNab

As I stepped through the wardrobe I touched nylon coats that slipped through my fingers like water. Oddly, I could also feel rough, wool jumpers that people would have worn in the Middle Ages. They felt scratchy and itchy to the touch. I was glad I wasn't wearing one of them!

I shuffled further in and caught a repulsive whiff of rubbish and pungent cow-dung. At the same time I breathed in a clean sterile scent, like the sort of smell you get when you open a pack of anti-bacterial wipes. I could hear the constant, ear-ringing gabble of the Middle Ages mixed with the silence of the future.

Then I saw people and buildings from the past and future: noble knights, high-tech domes, castles and space rockets. They appeared out of nowhere, and as they materialised I could feel a shock wave of air hitting me. I was extremely puzzled. What was happening?

I carried on, scuffing my shoes on the uneven floor. But then I tripped and fell flat on my face in a puddle of muddy water. I slithered around to see what I had tripped over. It turned out to be a small, blue wristband. I put it on. It seemed to fit perfectly.

Suddenly a whirlwind engulfed me. Blue, red and gold fiery stripes swirled around my body like a mass of rampaging bulls.

The strange whirlwind stopped. I seemed to have been transported to an earlier era. There were more medieval forts than space rockets and high-tech domes. I turned to the wardrobe and saw that it looked younger as well. It didn't have all the strange twisting, crippled cracks that it used to have. It was beautifully glazed with an amazing finish. I got the uneasy feeling that I didn't belong here.

I panicked and ran back into the wardrobe.

Upside Down Land
Joshua Moir

As I walked through the dusty wardrobe I felt something prickly brushing my head. There was enough light for me to see that the top of the wardrobe was covered in grass. I looked down at my feet. Cirrus clouds hid my shoes.

I stepped out into the sunlight. The sun was shining from below and mountains, trees and grass hung above me. Straight ahead was a town, but the roofs of the houses were on the ground and the doors were too high to reach. How could anyone live here?

I began to make my way through rows of houses that were balancing on their roofs and chimneys. They looked as though they might topple over. A group of people, walking on their hands, began to shout, 'You shouldn't be on your feet! The town policeman might catch you!'

I looked closely at them. They were perfectly balanced. I stared at my hands and feet and wondered how I could possibly do it. I put my hands on the sky, kicked my feet towards the grass and realised it was simple. There must be a magical force in this land.

I continued through the town and saw a sign up ahead, 'ꓕOdSʎ ꓕOMN MƎꓘƆOWƎS ƆⱯꓤƎꓒꓵꓕ HⱯNpMⱯꓘꓭꓲꓢ'

As I tried to read the sign, a man rode past me upside down on a bicycle. He called, 'Welcome to Topsy Town.'

I waved. My hands and arms were beginning to ache.

'Can you help me? I need to find my way back to the wardrobe.'

'You've come from the forbidden wardrobe?' he asked. 'I cannot take you there. I can only take you as far as the last chimney. That house belongs to Policeman Pug who stands guard over our town.'

It was a strange feeling, riding upside down. I felt the wind on my feet rather than in my hair. As we got closer to the wardrobe, I could see that someone was investigating it.

Policeman Pug!

Gaming Land
Rohan Patil

My Narnia is a gaming land. As I stepped into the wardrobe I felt the hardwearing feel of an engineer's suit combined with the burnt electrical smell of snapped wires. Walking through the wardrobe further I trod on slippery wires instead of feeling hard, smooth wood under my feet. The wires were red, green, white and black, which made the floor look like a ball of multi-coloured wool! 'This isn't right!' I thought.

I saw that there was a light ahead; not a few inches away where the back of the wardrobe ought to have been, but very far away. I bent down and felt the floor, which was all slick and slippery. Then I hit something hard. A TV! Out of nowhere! And the wires coming out of it led to an Xbox!

I walked a few metres ahead and bumped into another TV connected to a Wii, with loads of game discs next to it.

'My lucky day,' I thought.

Lying on the floor next to the Wii was a colossal iPad, much bigger than the one at home. That may be the future Apple!

Thinking I had a lot of choice, a big grin appeared on my face. A wave of excitement went through me and I nearly jumped for joy, but then I remembered that someone would be onto me if I did, so I just kept quiet! I couldn't resist having a go on at least one of the devices before someone caught me sneaking around!

Although I could taste the burnt electrical current in the air and hear the scary crackling of electricity ringing in my ears, I decided to have a quick go on the new iPad that none of my friends would have seen. So I switched it on and it came alive!

'Wow, it's 3D!' I said. 'What a machine!'

Dragon World
Freddy Purcell

As I went through the wardrobe I felt the scaly skin of a lizard-skin coat. I heard a clatter and saw a pile of bones of a devoured animal. I shivered and carried on cautiously.

A blinding light appeared ahead. I was confused as I was facing the back of the wardrobe! I stepped towards the light and saw a flock of dragons swooping and screaming as they dived down and snatched up unfortunate fish from the surface of the water, and swooped back up to the airy currents. The air tasted of life, birth, battles and death. I tripped over and, looking back, saw a twelve-headed, snake-like dragon ready to strike. I stood up in alarm and ran as fast as I could. I felt a dagger-like tooth scrape my ankle. I glanced back and saw the monster snarling and not bothering to move. I realised that it was only a carnivorous plant.

I carried on through the woods. Thank goodness there weren't any more of them gnawing on my ankles.

Suddenly I heard a rustle. I whipped around and saw a small, yellow dragon snarling, in what appeared to be a happy way. It leapt. I turned to run, but to my complete surprise it jumped onto my back and started purring. What amazed me even more was that it started to befriend me.

I soon got used to the cute, little dragon burrowing down my T-shirt and became friends with it. I started to feel hungry. It was as if the dragon could read my mind; he jumped happily out of my T-shirt and swooped up into the air and headed towards a lake. It was a magnificent sight.

All of a sudden the dragon dived at the speed of light into the water. He vanished and it made me worry. But then he reappeared with a fish in his mouth.

Sweet Land
Ryan Schumaker

As I step through the door I feel the sticky surface of a lollipop hanging in the wardrobe and smell melting, chocolate caramel. Going further in I step on tiny lollipops instead of grass, and hear them crunching under my feet. I can`t feel the smooth woodwork of the wardrobe any more. Instead I see a huge, magnificent, magical waterfall with purple water but, instead of stone forming the waterfall, it looks like cake. There is something extremely sticky and gooey on my feet. I start pulling and pulling, but I can`t get myself out of the sticky substance. I look down and realise I'm stuck in marshmallow fluff quicksand.

I pull some more, but the more I do this the further in I sink. The sticky and nightmarish goo is up to my neck and I can barely breathe because the marshmallow is crushing my lungs.

A sweet man comes over to help me. He grabs my arm and pulls me out, then asks what my name is. I tell him my name is Gregory.

We start walking. After walking for about half an hour we come to a sweet tree and climb up it. He tells me I can eat a liquorice leaf. I grab one and eat it; it tastes like heavenly goodness. He also says that not all of the sweets in this land are meant to be eaten – some can make you faint. He tells me to be careful for snakes on the tree because they blend in with the leaves.

Suddenly I see a leaf move. A snake bursts out of nowhere and chomps down on my sweet friend's arm and starts sucking him into his mouth! I scream in fear and think about running away and leaving him there, but then I think again and try to pull him out of the snake's mouth. It is no use; the snake has already eaten him whole, but with no time to feel sorry I jump off the tree and start running towards the waterfall.

I splash the weird purple water on my face and say to myself that this is a dream. I am trying to forget about the death of my sweet friend. I start to feel a little sleepy, then extremely sleepy. I realise it must have been the water, so I start to make my way towards the wardrobe, but there is no way out.

Liquorice Whiskers
Olivia Seaton

I step through the wardrobe; I feel the leather of dog leads and the tags of cat collars. I smell a mix of sweet sugar and cat litter.

Looking ahead there's a faint sparkling light in the distance, shining through the leads and collars. So I stand up and push through them. What I can see is a miracle – chocolate fountains!

I step further in and hear soft crunching under my Ugg boots. I reach down and touch the floor and I find small, sticky balls! I bring my hand up to my mouth to taste one. It is nice and sweet.

I turn my head and see strawberry chocolate, gummy bears, candy canes and lots of cats sleeping in the snow. There are so many sweet smells.

Then I decide that it is OK to take a few steps further in. I realise that this is my chance to have the sweets. They are everywhere! Then a cat comes round the corner; it looks gorgeous. It has a wonderful bushy tail and smashing, sparkly eyes.

He is white and ginger-striped. He also has a very droopy tail. The gorgeous cat prowls past and makes a little purr.

'The air smells of fish,' I say.

The smell is definitely coming from the cats because once some more cats pad round the corner, the air really, really stinks.

A few more cats appear. They rub against my legs. It is only now that I realise how long I have been looking at the smiling cats and the lovely sweets.

I sprint back to the lamp post with the glowing light inside it. As I run I think about what I am going to tell Susan, Edmund and Peter about my extraordinary visit to this epic and fun candy land.

Dream Land
Sophie Swale

As I stepped through the wardrobe I felt the feathery cotton of a pillow and heard the gentle sound of something billowing in the wind. I took another step and realised there is no wind in a wardrobe. 'Something seems wrong,' I thought, reaching out to feel the smooth surface of the back of the wardrobe. But it wasn't there!

My mouth started to water. I tasted the sweetness of a peach, ripe in the sun. 'Funny place to put a peach,' I thought.

I took some more steps forward and was so puzzled by the fact that there were peaches in a wardrobe (who on earth would do that?), that I tripped over something. As I fell forward I put my hands out expecting to bang my head on the back of the wardrobe. Instead I fell flat on my face.

'Why, the wood is all soft and dewy!' I muttered. Then a wonderful smell filled my nostrils, but it smelled just like grass. I looked down and realised it was grass! I glanced around. I wasn't in the wardrobe anymore. There were hundreds of trees, all loaded with fruit! I got up and picked a beautiful peach from a massive oak tree. I took a bite. It was remarkably refreshing. After that I felt too hazy to wonder why there were peaches growing on oak trees.

I took another look around and saw some squirrels skittering around, birds nesting in the trees and rabbits hopping about on the grass. Everything seemed so peaceful; too peaceful. I was feeling really sleepy now. I turned back to the wardrobe and suddenly remembered this wasn't my home.

'Oh dear,' I gasped. 'I must leave here.'

It was my last thought before I took a staggering step forward and collapsed. The peach core rolled onto the grass beside me, lying hidden in the grass, but my thoughts were elsewhere now. The world around me dissolved and a new one appeared. I would be in for a shock when I woke up.

Sweety-Treaty Land
Sam Trezies

As I walk further into the wardrobe I push aside the old, stained cooks' clothes and the well-worn chefs' hats. I step down hard on the wardrobe floor and instead of hearing the clunk of my boot, there's a crunching sound.

I keep my arms outstretched, expecting to feel the hard, solid back of the wardrobe. I walk on and see a tiny ball of light. I look down and find I'm actually walking on a path of Maltesers. I hurry on and the smell of luxurious liquorice wafts up my nose. Suddenly I see a magical land!

I hear the trickling of a caramel waterfall falling into a pool. Marshmallows drop on my head. I reach down and touch the grass; it feels weird, like liquorice. So that's what I can smell! I pick some up and taste it. It is delicious, better than anything you can buy in the shops. I look up and see lollipop trees in the distance and a towering mountain of jelly beans. I jump as a squishy gummy bear runs into me. I watch him bounce off to the caramel pool and dive into it. I walk over and dip my hand into the golden liquid.

'This is peculiar,' I think.

It feels so refreshing and relaxing. I glance up and see a pink gummy bear on a lilo, gazing up at the puffy, fluffy candyfloss clouds. I take a step back and look behind me, just in time, as a red strawberry lace truck with Liquorice Allsort wheels comes bouncing along the Malteser track.

I crunch along the track towards a pretty-looking gingerbread house, beside an old Curly Wurly trunked tree with green laces for leaves. I reach the house and knock on the door. It's answered by a Freddo Frog, who is wearing a Haribo ring on each hand.

'Hi,' I say.

Freddo slams the door aggressively in my face.

'How rude,' I think and wander off.

Year 5. Mrs Heaney's Set
Filling in the *Holes*

Imagine being accused of a crime you didn't commit and sent far away from home and into a hot, sweltering desert to dig holes, day after day.

This is the life of Stanley Yelnats in the novel *Holes* by Louis Sachar, and indeed the life in which Year 5 have immersed themselves this term.

Through reading, role play, performance and discussion, Year 5 have developed a better understanding of how the characters in this novel feel, think and act. This enabled and motivated them to write letters, diary entries and lists of punishments from different viewpoints.

We hope you enjoy our collection and that you too are inspired to read the amazing novel, *Holes*.

Illustration by Isobel Smith

Punishments
Sebastian Crow

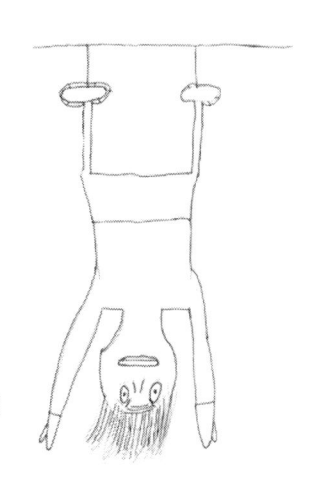

In the novel *Holes* Stanley gets sent to a juvenile detention centre for stealing a pair of sneakers. Not just any ordinary sneakers, Clyde Livingston's sneakers, which had been donated to an auction to raise money for homeless people. I think it was unfair for Stanley to be punished for a crime he didn't commit.

I have made up my own punishments for crimes committed in school.

Forgetting your homework
I sentence you to ten strokes of the headmaster's cane.

Stealing a friend's new pen
I sentence you to be dangled upside down for ten minutes.

Kicking a teacher in anger
I sentence you to five hard kicks back from the teacher you have kicked.

Breaking the fire alarm
I sentence you to dipping your toes into a fire for ten minutes.

Pushing someone down the stairs
I sentence you to suspension for two days and you must visit the person in hospital and bring the person flowers and chocolates.

Burping out loud in class
I sentence you to burping out a whole tune in Assembly.

Escaping from school
I sentence to you to attend Saturday School for one year.

I bet you are glad that you are not at my school. I would be a very strict headmaster.

Stanley's Diary
Kate Daniels

Today I had to dig a hole in the sweltering heat, again! We're not even digging where the warden should want us to! I hate this place. We had to dig a huge hole while the warden glared at us. Not to mention that while I was minding my own business, digging away, Zig-Zag hit me over the head with his shovel. For no reason! I guess he is jealous. Once more, he didn't help me up! He just said in a petty voice, 'Pick up your dirt, that's not my dirt, it's your dirt!' It was a tiny pile, which I had dropped when he hit me! What on earth is the world coming to?

Then, later on, Magnet and X-Ray ran in with a pile of sunflower seeds they'd stolen from the boss, who is not known for his good moods. They threw the seeds into my hole and complained that I should have caught them! Then it was just my luck that Mr Sir was passing by and saw the sunflower seeds I *didn't* steal. So, as always, I took the blame for something I didn't do. How very unoriginal! He took me to the warden, but she just got mad at him and put poison on his face.

When I got back, Zero had dug my hole. Life is

getting weirder and weirder.

This sucks. My food's gone mouldy, my bed stinks and I want to come home.

Yours irritably,

Stanley

P.S. The warden said I must have no breakfast for a week again, for no reason whatsoever.

Letter to Stanley
Alex Done

16 Shore Road

Silly Town

Texas

T53A2

6th October 2013

Dear Stanley,

I feel awful that you are being treated so badly in this camp. I wish you could come home tonight to watch *You've been framed* with me.

Dad thinks he has nearly found a way of recycling old sneakers. I feel really sorry for the old granny who lives next door to us. It must smell absolutely terrible out in the corridor! Hopefully Dad will have a breakthrough soon though. Who knows, maybe we will be rich someday.

We do hope you come home soon. We miss you terribly.

Lots of Love,

Mum and Dad

Stanley's Diary
Felix Fountain

Dear Diary,

I have just been hit on the head by a boy called Zig-Zag. I am so annoyed with people being unkind to me. I've tried to be nice to them but then I get hurt or hit on the head by a dirty shovel. All I want to do is lie in my bed. I don't have any proper friends and people call me Caveman.

I get really tired after digging a huge hole and sometimes I have no breakfast. I'm always worried a scorpion or a snake will bite me and no-one will come to help.

I want this year to go fast but it probably won't because I'm so unlucky. I hate Zig-Zig so much! Tomorrow I'm going to shove him in my hole and start throwing dirt and mud at him. I'm less kind to other people now but I'm getting fitter, which is good. I hope something good happens soon.

The warden used to be nice but now she is a witch. She doesn't even give us water.

See you tomorrow,

Stanley

Letter to Stanley
Hannah Gatehouse

>23 Avenue Road
>New Orleans
>Louisiana
>BA2 7AX
>14th August 1987

My darling Stanley,

I'm sorry you're having an awful time. Just one year left and so as long as we keep in touch you will be fine.

Mr Pedanski seems nice, but those weird nicknames for the other boys are really odd. About that boy, Barf Bag, and his bed; I promise when you get home I will make you a lovely bed! You will no longer have to smell the stench of sour milk either.

Your father is at work at the moment. He has been working so hard lately, but when he comes back I will tell him to write to you.

Good luck son!

All my love,

Mummy xxx ooo

Stanley's Diary
Lily Grosjean

Dear Diary,

I can't bear it here! Today I have been whacked on the head by a shovel, starved and worked to the bone. Zig-Zag was the one who hit me – I can't believe it. My head is gushing with blood and I'm in so much pain. I really want revenge but what can I do? Maybe I will whack him on the head tomorrow? UGGHHHH! I'm so annoyed! He was so selfish as well. When I fell he didn't even pick me up. He just stared at me.

'That's your dirt, pick it up,' he said, in his annoying voice.

I wish I was back at home in my warm, cosy bed. Right now I'm only getting three hours sleep. That's not enough. I need more!

Stanley's Diary
John Lowrie

Dear Diary,

What is it with Camp Green Lake making me dig a hole every day? If I don't get medical help soon I will die anyway, so I suppose it doesn't matter.

Why did Zig-Zag whack me over the head with his shovel? And why get so aggressive about some dirt? Now Zig-Zag is taking the mickey out of me. He's getting really jealous that I'm becoming better friends with X-Ray than him.

Tomorrow I'm going to whack Zig-Zag around the head and see if he likes it!

On a more positive note, X-Ray is really nice. He even said that if he found anything he would get me the day off! I think I'll do the same for him; he seems like a good person to have as a friend.

Punishments
Adi Mishra

In the novel *Holes* by Louis Sachar, Stanley (the main character) has been sent to a juvenile detention centre somewhere in Texas as a punishment for stealing Clyde Livingston's sneakers. This is a fake fact, he didn't even steal them!

Here are some punishments I have created for crimes committed by students in school.

Forgetting your homework

If this happens more than once, you will do the work while you are hanging upside down from the flagpole and being spun around.

Stealing a friend's new pen

All your pens will be snapped into tiny, tiny pieces and you will have to go out and buy some more.

Kicking a teacher

Your kicking leg will be tied up and you will be hung outside in the cold by your ears.

Burping out loud in assembly

You will be made to chew on a bar of soap.

Setting off the fire alarm

You will be tied up and squirted with high-power extinguishers.

Letter from Stanley
Arthur Pease

> Camp Green Lake
> Texas
> 1st June 2013

Dear Mum,

I kind of like it here. The only annoying downside is the food. It's not nice. Actually, it's awful.

I live in a lovely tent that kind of smells like rotten eggs. I suppose that is one of the other annoying downsides. I like it because it is so hot here; the temperature reaches up to forty degrees some days.

My very nice carer, Mr Pendanski, has a sunburned nose and a bushy beard. He lets us dig very big holes to get fit.

I like to get fit because then I will be nice and strong to dig all of the holes. I enjoy digging deep holes, especially climbing back out of them. At the end of the day, I have a nice cold shower to cool me down.

I have tea, then we go to bed at the late time of ten o'clock. We wake up at four in the morning in order to dodge the sun.

Hope you are well and lots of love,

Stanley

Letter to Stanley
Albert Perry

> 18 Bond Street
>
> Texas
>
> 31st April 2013

To my dearest Stanley,

How are you coping? I am missing you so very much. Dad is trying to prove you are innocent but to tell you the truth he isn't getting very far. What activities are you doing? I know you shouldn't have done what you did but you still shouldn't be there. You're my little Stan, Stan who still sleeps with Mr Cuddles. Sorry, I shouldn't embarrass you even if you are the only one reading this letter.

Dad is also working on what he is calling his *genius invention* but really he is trying to recycle old sneakers and get money for them. He has been hard at work downstairs in the cellar, which he calls his office and designing room. I haven't seen him in three days!

How is the digging going? Have you dug a hundred holes yet? It can't be that hard otherwise they wouldn't make you do it! Have you been rock climbing? You mentioned it in your last letter and I was wondering how it was going. Your teacher rang the other day to find out how you were; apparently your classmates are missing you. I don't know if this is true but I'm sure they must be.

How are your new friends? When you return home your friends can come and play and they can try my carrot, cucumber and cauliflower cake. I know you'll love it, your father does (well he will when he comes out of his makeshift office!).

The house is starting to smell of old trainers and sweaty feet, but I will sort that out before you come home.

See you soon.

Lots of Love,

Mummy

Letter to Stanley
Ella Reece

1 Nachos Lane
New York
Z9T QXZ25

Dear Stanley,

We are really missing you. Guess what? Your dad and I have just won the lottery so now we are rich! Rich! Rich! I hope you will carry on liking Camp Green Lake because unfortunately that's where you're going to stay! In three weeks our lottery winning mansion will be built. Hope you're not getting homesick because you'll be back with us in eighteen short months.

More about the lottery. Your dad went into Tesco, to the little table where you take a sheet of paper and a pen. He wrote down three random numbers and 'voila', we found out we'd won the lottery! Don't tell your friends; it's our little secret.

Once again I love you, my poochy poodle.

Lots of love, Mam and Dad. xxx

P.S. Don't hurt your back because that is the worst pain.

Punishments
James Reid

We have been reading the novel *Holes* by Louis Sachar. In the story a chubby boy called Stanley gets punished and sent to a juvenile detention camp called Camp Green Lake. In English we decided that this was an unfair punishment because Stanley didn't even commit a crime.

These are my punishments which I would give for crimes committed in King Edward's Junior School.

Forgetting your homework

You will be whipped ten times by Mr Taylor in Final Assembly and with your parents watching.

Stealing a friend's packed lunch

You will miss the next five lunches and have to gather stinging nettles to make stinging nettle soup, *without gloves on.*

Kicking a teacher in anger

You will be kicked back twice on each leg by every teacher in the school.

I bet you wouldn't want to commit a crime in *my* school!

Letter to Stanley
Jacob Robertson

> 28 Something Road
> Something Town
> Something County
> ABCD 123
> 6TH October 2013

Dear Stanley,

You are not missing much. Your Dad is still working on his project. He is trying to cook sneakers so it smells like burning rubber in the apartment. Yuck!

I hope you are behaving yourself and more importantly, I hope you can cope with digging a five foot deep hole every day. Also, I trust that you are eating and washing properly? You don't want to get sick.

Your Dad and I cannot wait for you to come home; we miss you terribly.

When you do leave, I wish you a safe journey home.

L.O.L.

Mom

Stanley's Diary
Jack Ruddock

Dear Diary,

It's been an absolutely horrible day. Zig-Zag whacked me in the head and I'm bleeding and hurting really bad. I feel very angry. I want to get revenge on Zig-Zag but what can I do? I've been sent back to my cot with no food, no water, no shower, like *I've* done something wrong! This place makes me so angry, I shouldn't even be here in the first place; I didn't steal anything.

I think Zig-Zag's jealous that me and X-Ray have a thing. Zig-Zag's just really crazy. I mean, he said to be quiet because he was watching television, when the television's been smashed to smithereens! There was nothing on for him to watch. Crazy lunatic!

I feel really depressed. He's taking the mickey out of me and I have no energy for it. I'm so tired.

Signed,

Stanley Yelnats IV

Stanley's Diary
India Sanderson

Dear Diary,

Today I was digging my hole and Zig-Zag hit me on the head with a hard metal shovel. I have a big cut and I am still bleeding. Zig-Zag just stood there; he didn't care. Maybe he's just jealous because I've been hanging out with X-Ray. Ouch! My head. I can't stop feeling the pain. I look like a dirty pig now, all covered in dried blood. When I got hit the only people who helped were Magnet and Mr Sir; he made a bandage for me.

My life is so bad here. They sent me to bed when my head was hurt, if you call it an actual bed. I am not looking forward to dinner, if you call it an actual dinner either. The food here is revolting. I am really tired, a tired and dirty pig. I wish there was a way I could get out of here; I can't stand it any longer. HELP!

Signed,

Stanley

Stanley's Diary
Isobel Smith

Dear Diary,

I am so angry! Today I got hit on the head with a shovel by Zig-Zag. To make it worse, he didn't even say sorry! I'm hungry, sweaty, tired, depressed and so angry I'm almost on fire! I wish I could just go home and see my Mom and Dad.

I'm writing this diary entry in a milky-smelling cot, that's how bad it is here. I think Zig-Zag hit me because he is jealous that X-Ray is looking after me and not him anymore. At the moment, the only people I like here are Zero and X-Ray, mostly Zero though. He's nice because he helped me dig my hole and he wasn't mean to me when I first arrived at Camp Green Lake, unlike the other boys.

Why do I hate Camp Green Lake so much? I'm too tired to answer that now.

Until tomorrow,

Stanley

Letter to Stanley
Florence Stockham

> 24 Salsberry Lane
> Spring Field
> SS77 4ZY

Dear Stanley,

I am missing you very much but it is very nice to know you are having fun and making friends. Dad thinks he is almost done with his sneaker project.

The landlord has, on many occasions, threatened to kick us out of the flat because of the smell! New people are coming and going, mainly going, because they are looking at the flats and not liking them. It must be the stench. It drives them away.

I have told the school that you are ill, because they keep poking their noses into our business. I hope you are settling in, but do not forget it is a punishment and you need to be learning from your mistakes.

I am good friends with a lady a couple of flats below. She has a son called Stanley too!

Lots of love,

Mom xxxxxx

Year 5. Mr Innes' Set

Illustration by Theo Hagan and Christopher Godwin

Can you become someone completely different? Can you change your world and live through someone else's eyes?

In your writing, you can do all this and more.

This term we have studied a range of stories and looked at the different types of dilemma you can experience as a reader. We have had a lot of fun exploring characters and their feelings through drama and role play.

In *Holes,* we have looked at the way Stanley's experience is portrayed and we have experimented with writing in the style of the author. We even wrote ballads about the life and times of Stanley's great-great grandfather and Kissin' Kate Barlow.

We have also looked at the ways writers can make their writing more descriptive and can really show their audience what is happening.

We have chosen our favourite pieces from this term for you to enjoy. We hope that you will have as much fun reading them as we did in creating them.

Happy reading!

Lost in the Wardrobe
Matthew Barclay

I walked into my room and my friend Humphrey was waiting for me, scoffing peanuts from a bucket.

'I need some more clothes,' I said. 'These smell like dog hair.'

I strolled towards the cupboard, opened the door and rummaged through my tops and trousers. The smell of clean fabric hit my nose instantly.

Oddly, at the back of the cupboard I noticed a glowing light. I took a closer look and saw it was a swirling, multi-coloured portal.

I stepped back in bewilderment.

The portal smelled like melting plastic. When I touched it, I felt a tingle in my foot getting stronger until it started hurting. The pain sucked my breath away. I fell to my knees, my eyes started to close and I thought I saw a light but it was just my lamp. My mind was going crazy. I couldn't think straight.

I stood up and saw three pathways, each one a different colour. One path was blue with blue trees, one was red with red trees and the last was green with green trees.

I tried to figure out what had happened. I felt dizzy

and tired. I knew I needed to find shelter but I had no idea where to go.

Finally, I made up my mind; I started down the third path. Everything I saw was green; even I'd turned bright green. It was misty and when I looked up at the sun it was green too!

Somewhere nearby, I could hear a river flowing steadily.

I kept walking until I heard a cry for help. The voice grew louder until I could see it was Humphrey. He had tears running down his face.

'What are you doing here?' I asked.

'I came to find you. I opened your drawer and a portal appeared,' he said. 'That's how I got here.'

We hurried down the green road, but where the portal had been was a blank space.

The Best Day Ever
Oliver Brook

I get to walk out of the tunnel. It's a cup match and it is also my first game for Manchester United.

The feeling is euphoric. The atmosphere is electric. The crowd are singing all their usual songs. I am wearing my favourite number seven shirt and playing alongside the best footballers in the world.

When the match starts, I get the ball and run with it towards the goal. I lash the ball with my right foot from thirty-five yards and it whizzes, swerves and dips into the top corner. The keeper was in no man's land.

The Stretford end go crazy; they are jumping up and down so I perform a cartwheel, a full front flip and then a back flip.

Manchester City kicks off and Sergio Aguero goes through on goal, but David de Gea palms it away and boots the ball up to the half way line. It gets to Cristiano Ronaldo, who shoots and scores.

Two nil to Manchester United!

Then we go through and score with John Terry. We just have time to kick off again and then the referee blows his whistle for half time.

After half time Manchester City kick off and score from eighteen yards with a blazing shot from Thierry Henry.

We go on to win a corner from a shot from Robin Van Persie, but then it is the last minute.

'Are we going to score again?' I think to myself. Wayne Rooney takes the corner and, from twenty yards, Jay Emanuel-Thomas scores with a bicycle kick.

The Stretford crowd jump up and down. The Manager is bouncing around madly. None of the team can believe it.

Just when we kick off, the referee blows his whistle: full time!

The pitch clears quickly, but in the stadium all the Manchester United players climb the steep steps to receive the FA cup.

I am the first to lift it! I receive my medal and look around me.

That is to be the first of many days with my team, and the start of a five-hundred-goal career.

Monkey Alert
Ben Dryden

I saw the guard opening the Eiffel Tower gates and I started to climb. I was swinging from handhold to handhold just like I do at home. When I reached the first floor the barman, shocked at my appearance, dropped the glass he was holding. 'That's strange,' I thought, 'my keeper never does that!'

I spotted a group of children and made funny faces at them. They pulled faces back at me, but the adults with them didn't see the funny side of it. They told me to get away and called the police. People come to look at me every day; what was different about today?

The police were there in a flash and began searching all around the Eiffel Tower in case I had escaped. They wanted to capture me and put me back in my cage. Oh no!

My photo was in the newspaper the next day with the headline 'Monkey Alert!'

I was enjoying being free so I decided to climb even higher. As I reached the second floor I could smell something familiar; tourists were eating a picnic and my tummy started to rumble. I had missed feeding time so I pinched a banana from them, but didn't understand why they were so angry.

Suddenly I heard policemen charging up the stairs to look for me. What no-one knew was that I was on my way to the very top of the tower. I had made a bed up there because it felt safe and I had a great view of Paris. I was swinging and swinging as if playing with my friends. I looked up and straight ahead of me was my bed; I climbed up to it and fell asleep.

When I woke up I was being carried by a young man. I wondered where I was going. My question was soon answered because he walked me straight back to the zoo. My cage was small, but I now had a French flag to decorate it. I couldn't climb as high, but I could still pull faces at everyone!

The Letter
Theo Hagan

Dear Mum,

The bus here was horrible. It smelled like sweat. The guard was facing me and he had a smirking smile on his face all the way. I had to have handcuffs on and my wrists were sweaty. I was so thirsty on the bus journey – they didn't give me a single drink. Out of the window, it was dry land and there wasn't any crop in sight.

When I arrived I couldn't see the lake. There weren't even any weeds. But there seemed to be something moving in a pit nearby.

When I got let out of my handcuffs my wrists were so hot and sweaty, but I was happy to be free of those hot hell chains.

There was a man eating some sunflower seeds. The man had a snake on his arm and when he moved his arm the snake moved with him. I found out his name was 'Mr Sir'. He was getting out two drinks. I was so thirsty that I desperately wished that one of the cans was for me, but it was only for the bus driver and the warden.

Mum, we have to dig a hole five feet wide and five

feet deep every day!

In every direction is the scorching desert, but luckily we've got clothing that reflects the heat off us.

It was horrible digging my first hole. I got blisters on my hand and there was blood everywhere. I had sand all over my face and in my mouth. I was exhausted because the shovels are so heavy and they aren't my size. We only get a small amount of water in our canteen each day, so my throat was bone dry and my legs were in agonising pain. My shovel just kept bouncing off the hard as steel desert ground and the vibrations wrenched my arms.

I don't know if I can dig another hole.

Sincerely,

Your only son,

Stanley xxxooo

The Farmhouse
Ebony Hammond

One late evening, when the sun was slowly sliding down the sky, I began my last duty of the day - feeding the animals. It was one of my favourite jobs.

All of a sudden I heard a little voice.

'Who is there?' I shrieked.

'It's just my mind,' I was thinking, but then I heard it again.

'Stop it!' I shouted at the shadows.

I suddenly realised it must be one of the animals.

'But animals do not talk,' I thought, 'yet maybe it is true and animals *can* speak. It's only me and the animals here.'

As I fed them one by one, I realised they were all lying down, looking at me. It made me worried.

Then all of a sudden the horses started talking to me. I did not know quite what to do, so I spoke back.

'Er, hello horses. H-how long have you been able to talk?' I asked nervously.

As quick as lightning, every single animal in the yard started talking, even the rat, and he was under the floorboards.

So, every day when I woke up I went to speak to

the horses. It made my life easier because they were able to tell me when they were unhappy, didn't want to be ridden or even if they were going to throw me off!

After a few weeks, I became very good friends with all of them. I started to understand horses and the nature of them.

I love speaking to my animals; it is the highlight of my day.

Sometimes I wonder how it would be without my animals to talk to.

Lions
Evie Handel

I wandered in the lonely woods,
Looking for a friend to share my goods.
A friend to care, a friend to share,
A friend to follow me everywhere.

The shadowy light played tricks on my eyes
I was in no mood for a surprise.
It felt like this chapter of my life would never end,
These woods were so lonely I needed a friend.

I felt like there were eyes upon mine
That sent a shiver down my spine.
I heard the rustle of leaves behind me.
Was it the wind or someone kindly?

I saw a figure under the spreading tree.
I had the feeling it was looking at me.
I went closer …
She came closer.

We heard a sudden cry from the heart of the woods.
She ran away and I just stood,
Waiting in desperation for her return.
It felt like a hard lesson to have to learn.

I was startled by every rustling sound.
My heart, I could really feel it pound.
Then, again I saw her looking at me;
I knew it was my destiny.

The Pig, the Boy and the Curse
Iyshea Hender

Elya was fifteen and the girl of his dreams,
Myra was fourteen and lonely it seems.
Wishing to marry her, he asked her dad,
Then realised he had a rival, which made him feel sad.

So Myra's dad said, 'The winner will be
The one who returns the heaviest pig to me.'
Elya was worried and unsure what to do,
So he went to Madame Zeroni to ask for a clue.

'I will help you,' she said to him,
'But be warned – Myra is very dim.
Take this pig,' Madame Zeroni said,
'I know it is weak and nearly dead.'

'Take it up the mountain every day
And be very careful of the rocky way.
Let it drink from the fast-flowing river,
And every day t'will get bigger and bigger.'

So he took the pig up the mountain each day
Throughout the sunny month of May.
He had a bath. How could he possibly win?
And so he went to Myra's for the weigh-in.

But alas the pigs weighed exactly the same,
So nobody won that particular game.
Myra, unable to choose between Elya and Igor,
Decided to select by number and nothing more.

'I no longer wish to marry her,' Elya admitted,
'Because she is so very dim-witted!'
So leaving the pig, far, far behind,
He walked off, miserable, in heart and mind.

Forgetting that, to prevent Zeroni's curse,
He had to remember to quench her thirst.
He packed his bags and travelled abroad,
Marrying beautiful Sally, to whom he was allured.

The Big Prank
Luke Hepworth

'We're late. Run!' shouted Lewis, as they charged through the school gates and into school.

Joe and Lewis rushed into their classroom, slamming the door against the wall.

'You know the rules, boys; you've been at this school a long time. No running!' said Mrs Wilkinson crossly. 'Go outside and walk in properly!'

Then the bell rang.

'Time for our plan,' said Joe.

They hung back at the end of the line into the science class, then turned and sneaked down the stairs and hid in the cleaning cupboard.

After fifteen minutes, the coast was clear. Joe and Lewis tiptoed out of the cupboard, down the corridor and pushed open the door to the playground. They sneaked to the flower bed and dug a hole.

'Look at these big, fat, juicy, slimy worms!' said Joe.

'Let's get fifty!' Lewis giggled.

The boys ran down the stony path and very quietly pushed open the back door to the kitchen. They crawled very slowly and quietly on their hands and knees and hid under the counter next to the stove where the cook was working.

They waited, holding their breath and praying she would not hear or see them. Finally she left the stove. Climbing out from under the counter, Joe and Lewis quickly put all the juicy worms into the pot of spaghetti and mixed it up with the wooden spoon.

They crept back to their hiding place but then the cook turned. They were sure she had seen them.

'Stay still!' whispered Joe. They were both sweating heavily.

'Phew!' Lewis said under his breath.

***

The bell rang for lunchtime. Everybody rushed through the doors. They sat down at their tables and looked at the lunch menu. The person next to Joe and Lewis said, 'Great! It's spaghetti!'

Everybody queued up to get their portion of spaghetti, including the teachers. They sat back down and twisted their pasta onto their forks.

Then everybody screamed.

'Aaargh!' The headmaster spat worms into Mrs Wilkinson's face.

'Whoever did this is in big trouble!' he thundered.

The City at Night
Izzy Hughes

The party had just finished, my friends were gone. I was nine-years-old now; it wasn't my bedtime, although it was nine thirty. Wait – where were my mum and dad?

'Mum! Dad!' I cried, 'this can't be right: they were here a minute ago!'

I'd have to walk back to the hotel, in the dark, with no-one looking after me. I couldn't do it! All the same, I slowly started to walk home.

But then it came to me: 'I might get killed, like grandad did in this city! Oh no!'

Now I felt even worse. I heard a sound and saw a shadow behind me. It wasn't my shadow.

'Who's there?' I called, 'Come out! You'll regret this!'

I didn't feel tough; I felt scared. What if it was a murderer? I heard a squeak in the background. The shadow moved. Where was it now?

Then I realised there was an alleyway. I could see the shadow. I crept towards it with my bag in my hand. I could use it as a weapon. There was nothing else I could do. I would try hitting the creature, for I didn't know what it was.

Then I saw one dirty, bare foot sticking out from the corner of the alleyway and I was terrified, so frightened that I ran. I must have run for about half a mile, at least it felt like that far because I was gasping for breath.

At last I was in the city centre, with all the lights on the buildings, the amazing New York lights. Cars were driving past and it was like the day but dark.

Now I had to go down a final alleyway – the scariest bit of all. There were beggars everywhere asking me for money but I just avoided them.

Then I was on a quiet street where everyone was looking at me. I didn't know why they were staring at me. Was it because I looked weird? Or because I had my dress tucked into my underwear?

By the time I had finished faffing with my clothes, I was at the hotel. Mum was pleased to see me and I was very pleased to see her.

Well that was a night!

The Dream
Roxy Livingstone

The wind whipped my salty, tear-stained face. My best friend, Ezra and I were literally *dying* of exhaustion. We had been running away from this completely *evil* wolf, which I was sure would have savaged us if we hadn't climbed up, up, up and up onto the branch of a dead tree.

I hung onto the branch for dear life. The gorge was below me, just waiting to swallow me up. My hands were numb with cold, but I was sweating badly. My hands were slipping; I felt like I would fall at any moment, so I flattened myself against the cold, hard, wet surface of the branch.

'EZRA! EZRA! Where are you?' I looked around me.

Ezra was gone. She had fallen. My heart plummeted like a rock in water. Beneath me I could hear the rushing of the waves, feel the salty spray on my face. My nightmares had come true. I felt sick and dizzy, dizzy and sick.

'CRACK!' The branch snapped clean in two and I found myself falling ... falling ... falling into the inky blackness. Then I was floating, floating up into space.

Then, 'CRASH!' I hit something hard.

It was quite soft actually, soft for the amazing noise it made, anyway. I slowly opened my crusty eyelids. I blinked once, twice, and then I shut my eyes, pinched myself hard, and opened them again; but every time I did this, still the same sight met my eyes.

I was sitting, shocked, on the floor of my bedroom, half asleep. I think I must have fallen out of bed, because I remember hitting something hard. I presume it was the floor – I have wooden floorboards.

But I can tell you one thing: from that day onwards, until this very day, I have been thinking of what might have happened to Ezra, because I haven't seen her since the dream.

My Dream
Jim McAllister

We are twenty-one nil up at the fifty-sixth minute; the crowd is cheering my team on but Ferguson is not. He is shouting at us.

I am playing with Messi, Ronaldo, Neymar and Ibrahimovic. I am the captain of the team. The other team is West Ham. My strip is black and white and it is the league final.

Do you know how very scary it is? How you get very sweaty, very claustrophobic, especially when it is late at night?

I am standing at the half way line when it happens: Messi passes to Neymar, then Neymar chips the ball to me. I jump and flick it round with the back of my right leg then bicycle kick it. The ball rebounds off the crossbar and ends up in the bottom corner, bouncing gently up and down behind the puzzled keeper.

I have scored my first goal and there is a massive roar from the crowd! Even Ferguson is jumping about! I do a full flip backwards, better than Peter Crouch's celebration. The players jump on me.

'Yeah!' I shout.

Then we score another goal and another! We are now twenty-four nil up at exactly the sixtieth minute.

'We are not going to lose!' I shout.

We are thirty nil up then and six more goals up at the seventieth minute.

But what's that feeling? I feel a cold shiver up my back and I almost pass out, but luckily I get over it. Then suddenly a few minutes later, I get the feeling again, and this time my legs go from under me and I fall to the ground.

Everyone crowds around me; it is petrifyingly scary. They pick me up and I have to be carried off on a stretcher made of hard, uncomfortable plastic like the ones you see on TV.

***

When I wake up and look around, it is the middle of the night. The football posters around my room stare at me with Messi, Neymar and Ibrahimovic's eyes.

I feel the sweat on my skin.

'MMMMMMUUUUUUUUUUUMMMMMM!'

Destroyed
Jack McGladdery

I arrived home from school, put the key in the lock and turned it slowly. Once the door was open, I saw that my house had been trashed; it was as if a flaming meteor had hit my precious home!

There was water everywhere. It was coming from all directions out of the kitchen ceiling. The television had been smashed on the floor. I felt the howling wind slither past my face. Slowly, my eyes got blurry.

Suddenly I heard a loud crash! The wall collapsed and dust went everywhere, in my eyes, up my nose, into my ears. Yuck! It was horrible. I felt like I was going to die.

When I opened my mouth, I tasted bitter dust. I smelled a horrible smell, as bad as sour milk, which I followed to the kitchen.

Once I got into the ghastly room, I froze in shock. The table was snapped in half and the fridge tipped over. All the food was scattered on the wet floor.

'How am I going to survive?' I thought to myself. The house had turned into a bombsite.

I wanted to see what sort of state my room was in, so I walked out of the kitchen and climbed the stairs.

Splinters on the banister caught my skin. When I finally got to the top of the stairs, I was relieved.

I could hear running water, so I headed into the bathroom and quickly turned off the bath taps.

In the silence, I rushed to my room. My bed was broken and there was a massive hole, right in the middle of the floor.

I remembered I had left my phone downstairs so I ran out of my room to get it, but suddenly noticed a large patch of blood on an undamaged wall.

It was then that I thought to myself, 'Oh no! Will I ever see my parents again?'

Barcelona vs Real Madrid
Adrian Moayedi

It was time for kick off; Barcelona started. I passed to Messi and we passed around to each other and went up the pitch as a team. We were struggling like a fly trying to get away from a spider's web, but their defence was rock solid; we couldn't break through them. We had a plan, a plan like never before, something totally different from the usual moves. The magnificent plan was to tire out the defence in the first half so in the second half we could outpace them and score. It was a dull first half for the sleepy audience.

In the second half, which was going to be an excellent one, I tackled Bale and did a lovely pass to Neymar, who sprinted like Usain Bolt to the box. Neymar went through two defenders like they were not there and curled the ball into the box, exactly to my foot. I volleyed the ball into the top right corner.

Later, I stole the ball from Ronaldo and sprinted to the corner, going through three players. I was too speedy; I got ready to cross but Sergio Ramos kicked my foot and broke it.

'No,' I told myself, 'I am still going to play, even if I

have broken my foot.' Ramos received a red card.

Zlatan took the free kick. Amazingly, it came to me but slightly behind. I turned and did a bicycle kick with my broken foot, putting it into the top left corner.

Real Madrid took a bad shot but Valdes saved it, as if a five-year-old girl had had a shot against him. He threw the ball to me, and I was on the halfway.

I heard the commentators say five seconds left. I didn't know what to do; there was no point in passing so I just shot from there. The ball soared really high but like magic it came down and into the open goal.

I ripped off my shirt, jumped and punched the air. I had scored a hat trick!

The Lonely Minotaur
Kathleen Nicholas

The Minotaur sits alone in the darkness,
Waiting for companions, controlling his sadness.
His bulging stomach is rumbling, his fur is freezing,
Only to find that a friend comes creeping.

At every corner you will learn,
You will find something frightful at every turn.
Puzzles and riddles are always there,
Mixing your mind and twisting your hair.

The newcomer finds his way through the labyrinth,
As fast as light and agile as a mantis.
His footprints echo through the gloomy maze,
But the Minotaur thinks he is not insane.

The Minotaur stands up with all his might.
He puts on his ring, shining greatly and bright.
His friend approaches with something sharp,
Leaving a mark on the Minotaur's heart.

The Minotaur lies in sorrow and tears,
Knowing that the end of his life is here.
His friend leaves in pride and more.
This was the story of the lonely Minotaur.

The Greatest Adventure
Filip Oczko

I went mountain biking one afternoon, just behind our house. My front wheel started jumping on the rocky land and I eventually stopped near a stream to take a swig from my water bottle.

Just as I was leaving, I saw a bright yellow glow between the trees. I dumped my precious bike on the ground and started pushing through the bushes. The branches scratched my face. The glow became brighter and brighter as I forced my way through, and then I saw a cave.

I crawled into the cave and saw a sparkling yellow crystal. Water dripped off the ceiling, but I kept on exploring further into the cave.

As I went deeper, I suddenly saw a spaceship! It was giving off a faint, grey light.

I went up to it and tried to open the door, but it was stuck. My fingers slipped off the rough metal and I fell backwards.

BANG! My back hit the rock. I tasted the bitter tang of blood.

After a few moments, I saw a small hole in the ship's underside. I crawled over to it and climbed in with all the strength I had left.

Suddenly I gained back amazing energy.

Looking around, I saw a broken down door. I went through and saw hundreds of containers. Inside of each of those containers were more of those weird, glowing crystals.

I took one of the crystals and carried it back home. I examined it and it didn't seem very special at all, apart from the yellow glow.

I turned on my computer to find out where the science lab was and when I found it I went straight there. I asked my friend who worked at the lab about the crystals and he said they were really rare.

He took the crystal from me and investigated it for a few weeks. Then when he phoned me up he told me that they were normal crystals.

'Oh well,' I thought, but it was still the greatest adventure!

Yellow Spotted Lizard
Conrad Perry

Clunk, clunk, clunk. Metal hit earth.

Exhaustion, absolutely bone-breaking exhaustion. I felt nothing in my arms and legs but my head was spinning in crazy circles under the boiling sun.

The sudden pain I felt was agonising, unbearable, like billions of red hot needles. I fainted.

Everyone heard me, everyone saw me, so they rolled me back to the tent. They made sure the coast was clear and no-one was watching.

'What happened?' Squid bellowed.

'What, how did – what's happening?' I asked.

'We all saw you faint out there, man,' said X-Ray.

'Why are your socks so short?' coughed Magnet.

'Huh?' I was confused. I looked down at my feet. Magnet was right; my socks were short. I didn't know why Magnet was looking at my feet.

'Maybe when they got washed they shrank,' I said.

'No way,' Magnet replied. He was right: there was a green-looking bulge on my skin and it was making my socks short. I'd been bitten!

They had each been given a paperback: *Guide to*

Lizards when they arrived. Squid took out his copy.

'Right: lizards, poisons, infections ...' He thumbed the pages to infections. It came up with people being poisoned and what they looked like afterwards. The bulge on my leg looked exactly like the picture under 'Yellow-Spotted Lizard'.

'Uh oh,' Zero had finally spoken.

'It means you're dead,' Armpit said.

'What? Why?' I asked.

'Their bites are poisonous,' Armpit replied. 'If I were you, I'd lie in the warden's hammock.'

So I wrote a letter to my mum, saying that I was dead. I licked the seal on the envelope and handed it to Magnet to send. I saluted him and lay in the hammock. Everyone went back to work.

I chose a bad time because the warden saw me.

'What are you doing?' she screamed.

'Um, I got bitten by a yellow-spotted lizard and I'm going to die.'

I showed the warden.

'Don't be daft: that's a *green*-spotted lizard bite! Since you lay in my hammock, that's a hole to dig, ten feet in every direction now!' she yelled.

Spike's Surprise
Oscar Rudd

It was a Monday morning and I was chatting to my best friend, James, when I heard a rather unpleasant high-pitched noise. It sounded like my pet rat, Spike.

Suddenly I remembered that earlier that morning I had sneaked him into my bag! I knew I had to act fast.

I instructed James to look out for Mrs Scolding, as I retrieved Spike from my bag. I didn't want Mrs Scolding to know about him as she got cross very easily and I wanted to get revenge ...

As soon as Spike was in my hands, I told James to follow me into the corner of the cloakroom. I whispered eagerly that I had a cunning plan.

James and I returned to the classroom and I signalled him to scamper over to Mrs Scolding's chair and put Spike under the cushion!

'Phew!' James sighed when he had finished. 'I'm glad that's over!' he whispered in my ear.

After a few minutes, the bell rang for the first lesson and James and I rushed back to our desks before Mrs Scolding arrived.

As she stomped in, she shouted, 'Class, Maths!'

and screamed out the eight times table.

'Eight fours are thirty-two, eight fives are forty,' the class droned.

A few times tables later, Mrs Scolding stomped over to her chair and launched herself onto the seat. Her face changed colour and she let out a massive scream.

'AGH! There's a rat on my chair!' she bawled and rushed out of the classroom.

Spike let out a terrified squeal and ran under my desk. The class erupted with laughter.

The headmaster ran in, purple-faced, and demanded to know who was responsible for this deed, whilst the English teacher calmed a sobbing Mrs Scolding.

'If nobody owns up to this terrible crime, it's a whole class suspension,' he declared.

There was a long silence then Spike started to whimper. He made a dash towards the feet of the headmaster, who turned and ran.

Grabbing Spike, I shouted, 'Let's go!' and we all ran laughing from the classroom.

Sky's Adventures
Aoi Seiki

Another miserable day in my cage. My wings feel stiff and cramped. The air feels stuffy. I look in the mirror; I see lots of beautiful sky and blue feathers but I look so miserable. I try my toys but I don't feel any better.

My owner has forgotten to close the door! I slowly push it open. I hop to the door, one hop at a time. I'm out of my cage! I am excited but a little bit scared. I fly to the sofa. The window is open! I can't believe my luck. My name is Sky and that's where I am going!

I fly to the tallest poplar tree. I hold on to the branch with my claws; the breeze is making the branches sway from side to side. I can see the old buildings in Bath. I can see for miles and miles. I can see a robin on another tree eating some cherries. I can hear the soft breeze rustling the brown leaves. It is so beautiful. I fly up; it is breath-taking. It is amazing to be free! I can fly anywhere – I could soar up to the far horizon.

Is anyone going to bring some food? Do I have to find my own? I eat some of the cherries. Way better than stiff seeds. Why didn't I come out earlier?

Now it's getting dark and it's too cold. There's my lovely house. I wish I could go home but the doors and windows are shut against me. The branches feel crunchy and stiff with frost, like ice-cream. The twigs move like hands and try to catch me with their sharp claws. I ask the robin if he wants to come home as well. The robin puts his head on one side and then flies away.

Who's that coming? It's my owner! What is she holding? It's a cage with another bird in. Just then my owner looks up and she notices me in the tree. I fly into her open hands.

It is always darkest beneath the lighthouse.

Year 6. Mr MacFarlan's Set

Objects of Mystery

This year, as in the past, my set has been studying the incredible stories in Geraldine McCaughrean's *A Pack of Lies*, in which humble, apparently insignificant items acquire miraculous properties in the imagination of one the book's leading characters. Our challenge – including my own – was to write a much condensed poem in the same tone and 'flavour'. Judge for yourselves if we have succeeded or not.

Illustration by Lily Page

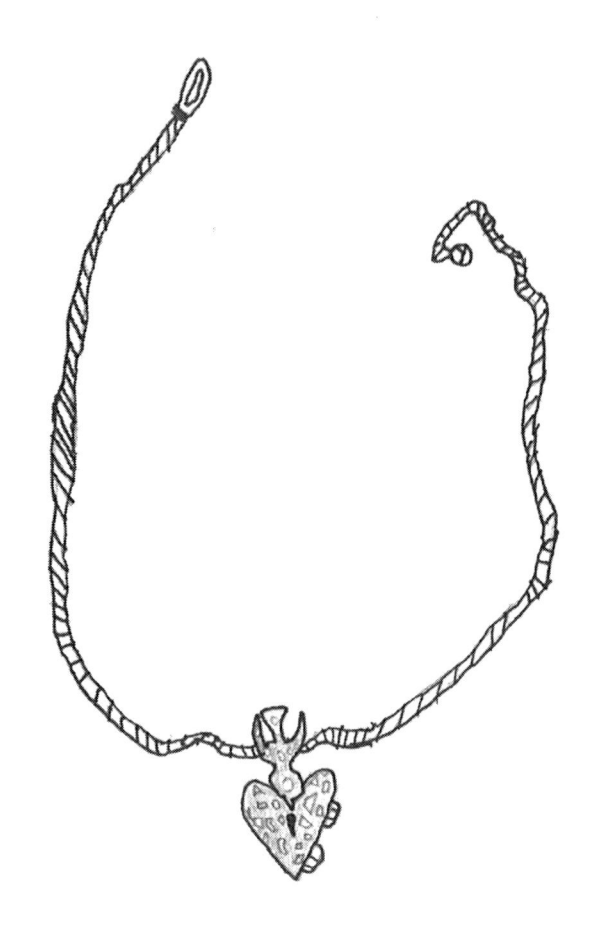

Illustration by Orlando Alford

The Acme Thunderer
Mr Mac

It sits snugly on the table like a drum with an ear trumpet, eavesdropping.

The matt black plastic of this infamous whistle sets it apart instantly.

Pick it up, though, and the smooth curves and edges slip comfortingly into the palm. With this whistle, I am somebody; in charge.

Its lightness is deceptive: every gram feels solid - double the weight. Take a ruler to it and the measurements don't show its power.

Which is why, amongst hundreds of other items on the bric-a-brac table, it remains anonymous, until ...

... a small child, ignoring his mother, puts it to his lips and blows!

And then, in an instant, we are treading the silky turf of Wembley and Hurst is again making history with the last kick of the game.

So, Acme Thunderer, thunder on!

Jug of Wonders
Phoebe Aisher

The plain milk jug sits alone in the cupboard waiting for someone to grab it once again.

But when you take a closer look it really has a story to be told.

The silky white casing glistens in the lamp light, waiting for a glimpse of the smooth creamy milk.

Its lettering stands out, out of the jug; the black, dark colour really shows what it actually is.

If you touch the outside you get a shock with the coldness that it carries amongst itself.

What the jug wants is to be used and see your hand reaching out to take it onto the long treacherous table.

The weightless glazed jug comes out of the dark and dismal cupboard, but when you pour the fresh cold milk it seems to feel much heavier than it is.

Likewise the height of it is small. This shows the little amount that it is used.

Which is why out of all the nooks and crannies of objects, I choose the Jug of Wonders.

The Locket of Secrets
Orlando Alford

From the rose-gold bird with the diamond eye,
hanging from the yellow string,
in order to tell its story,
the true key one must bring.

The diamond encrusted heart,
with the coal-black key shaped hole,
bonded with eternal love,
to the joyous love-struck soul.

Locket, the eternal guard,
with your woeful tale,
in the very darkest hour,
your faith in love will never fail.

The School Shoe
Sophie Bassil

It lies on the ground keeping your foot safe away from danger.

Its colour is as black as night. It catches your eye with your first glimpse.

When you take your first steps, your mum and dad are sure to buy the school shoe, as it's waiting to be moved.

Its texture is bumpy and its heart shines in the sunlight, but it is never old and it will always stay clean.

As you're wanting to take it off the shelf, your parents say it's a good fit.

The black shiny shoe shines in the night, gleams in the day, but you will never ever throw it away.

The Telephone
Adam Baxter

Shaped like a pill, the telephone is encrusted with twenty-one little buttons, each with a different function.

The shiny black and dull greys complement each other nicely.

As you pick it up it feels smooth and sleek.

The phone may be small but it holds the unfathomable power to contact anyone anywhere.

It is very heavy for 14cm long but that's because of its power.

As you dial a number, the innocent beep-bleep-blip-blop-blop hides the telephone's incredible properties.

The Pale Pink Pencil Pot
Elsie Berry

The roundness of the rim, the petals shaped almost like roses.
Flowering.
The pale pink pot, like a ballerina.
Bursting out.
The smooth underneath, the bumpy flowers.
Opening up.
Light as air, heavy as metal.
Floating.
As tall as a tower for Thumbelina.
Growing.
It dances on the shelf, charming little eyes with its little flowers.
WATCHING.

The Silver Bottle Opener
John Claydon

The eerie, smooth handle with that downwards point gives it a slight uplift.

The shiny iron-silver gives it a bit of a glare, but it still can't intimidate you.

The point of the long handle gives you just enough adrenaline to feel a tinge of fear.

It makes the hairs on the back of your neck stand on end.

It could lash out of its own accord at any moment and slice your finger.

The Shiny Bladed Scissors (That happen to have a personality and a *very* shiny blade!)
Thomas Crawford

Lying in a drawer or in a pencil case waiting for me to take you out.

The sharp blade can cut anything. Anything!

It can cut a fifty pound note and its value goes.

It can cut someone's hair when they are not looking and their temper goes.

The texture of the blade is smooth, smooth as a window pane fresh out of a warehouse.

I also love to squeeze your hand as you slice through the paper.

The bright colours that nobody recognises stand out for me.

Scissors are wonderful things!

The Drinks Mat
Alex de Beer

Its shining curved edges are like a flower staring right at you.

The dark blue on the outside and light blue on the inside give it the best contrast with the flowers and hot-air balloon coloured white, yellow, red, green, black, orange and pink.

It stands out amongst other things as it brightens up the shop.

Pick it up – it covers your hand.

You can feel that you can do anything.

It's light and heavy at the same time –

every gram counts as the scales settle.

A kid ignoring the rule – Don't touch anything! – comes up and puts his drink on the drinks mat.

We all go back to the time when this ancient relic was made.

The Elemental Mug
Max Entwisle

It hangs upon the mantelpiece, the handle strong and proud.

The colours of the elements depicting stories, stories of my family.

You pick it up.

You feel the elements flowing through the mug and vanishing into you.

Instantly you realise how many tough challenges my family has gone through.

It feels as light as a feather, although made out of the heaviest clay in the market.

Its height is way off the height of danger through its life.

The Red, Red Pencil (it's so, so red!)
Cecilia Gerber

A long thin pencil coming closer and closer to the end – a large pointy spear.

The golden rim of the rubber dazzles in the light and gleams like twinkling cat's eyes at night.

The eerie blood red paint drips down the writing tool.

It feels smooth at first but once you let your fingers run across the engravings it gives a rough, tough feel.

When you pick it up it feels feathery light but is solid and stands its ground.

It's tall and fierce yet thin and weak.

Sitting lonely on a dusty shelf waiting to be picked up and write yet another story.

The Magic Pot
Ammar Hassan

It looks like a painting on a bowl with fantastic art work.
The dark brown makes it the odd one out from all the other objects.
When you touch it, it's so smooth, like a snake's skin.

Oh pot, what secrets do you hold? Let me see! Let me see! Oh pot, where is the key?

The curves fit in perfectly with the smoothness.
The weight is unbelievable; it looks light but is as heavy as a rock.

Oh pot, what secrets do you hold? Let me see! Let me see! Oh pot, where is the key?

The Secret of the Screwdriver
Cameron Kelly

Imagine you were a screwdriver, shaped like the handle of a pistol.

It feels like a smooth coconut and is as graceful as a tortoise.

It has the power to tighten the bolts holding Lewis Hamilton's F1 car together, even though it is small and orange.

When you drop it into your beautiful toolbox, it clangs like a steel post being dropped in a scrap yard.

It sticks to your hand with an indescribable grip.

You know that it would be a disgrace if you threw it away.

That is the secret of the screwdriver.

The Wooden Box
Megan Lintern

The curves of the wood glint in the light, while the clasp is a shadow of mystery.

The distinctive wooden base is as strong as an ox, able to stand strong until the end.

The gold of the metal shimmers silently, as the red-brown surface is littered with marks of age.

As you pick it up, your fingers slip comfortably around it to meet the grooves and indents.

A space inside, three centimetres high, willing to hold memories and dreams.

The everlasting experience of a great event floods eagerly inside, knowing it is safe.

Look closely and see small indents in the metal and spirals in the wood, made with love and passion.

Which is why, amongst all the other objects, this small, handmade box draws you towards it.

Then, it is summoned from the shadows, and cradled in a child's hands,

ready to guard secrets again.

The Carnival Candle
Lily Page

The smoke rises into the dark moonlit sky, like a black cape sweeping over the moon.

The sweet glow of gold warms the empty world all around.

The shape of the smooth wax spreads like pouring warm chocolate onto a marshmallow to roast on a fire.

The weight of it is light, but the dripping hot, scalding wax, makes it a lot heavier.

The flame dances like a gymnast, flipping and twirling in the evening light.

It stands there, using the power of the flame to make the whole room come alive with the glow of The Carnival Candle.

It fills the cold damp empty room full of wonders to be seen.

That's why, out of all the heart beating things on the table, I choose The Carnival Candle.

The TV Remote
William Pinder

The TV remote is on the table waiting to control the TV with its menacing buttons.
As complicated as an aeroplane cockpit,
and as smooth as glass.
The master of all channels.
It's just an everyday object.
Or is it?
Thin and powerful, the TV has to obey its every command.
It feels light in the hand, yet every gram feels solid.
When you pick it up, you can feel the shiny and curved edges like an uncut conker.

The Key
Wilfred Saumarez-Smith

It lies firmly guarding its territory of unlocking a new world.

The soft, shiny metal reflecting the surrounding of its surface telling everyone it's in charge.

Pick it up and grip it firmly. Think of all the things it's done and all the things it's been through.

Heavy with memories and dreams that slip right into your hand.

Small but powerful.

The Pencil
Max Sears

It rolls unevenly on the table, lurching around, impossible to make still.

It seems impossible to catch – as if its past has made it alert.

The black and yellow colouring is almost hypnotising. It seems to try and make you come closer.

If you pick it up, its rough texture seems to grab you to let it go.

But it is tricky: it almost tells you to gently put it down, like a small king.

Sometimes it weighs you down, sometimes it is as light as a feather.

Amongst all the other items nobody notices or knows its story until a little boy picks it up and plunges into the darkness of 1999 New Year's Eve.

The Coin
Alex Weimar

I walk along the street with my head down because I have to go to school.

I see something gleam in the dark gutter.

My face lightens up like a street lamp.

The golden surface reflects off my backpack.

It is chocolate fuel so I can buy chocolate with it.

It rolls down the gutter into the drain and I catch it.

It jumps out of my hand.

I start crying because I haven't had a chocolate in years!

Illustration by William Pinder

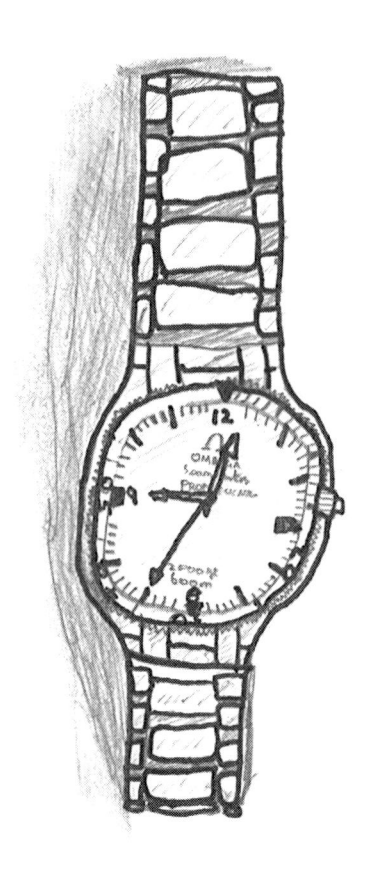

Year 6. Mrs Hardware's Set

We chose to create some poetry as an extension to a piece of comprehension entitled, *The Dragon in the Coal Shed*.

The aim was to envisage something quite extraordinary that appeared in a very ordinary place e.g. the fiery dragon asleep in a coal shed at the bottom of the garden.

Illustration by Jemima Tollworthy

The Monstrous Troll
Emma Botterill

I drove across the toll bridge,
When something caught my attention.
A mighty monstrous troll,
That made my body fill with tension.

His eyes were red, his skin was rough,
I looked at him with a stare.
I thought he'd run away,
But he stayed right there.

He was solemn and lifeless.
I knew he wanted to go home.
He was most of all lonely.
This troll was surely most defiantly ALONE.

I looked at him again,
And saw he had some tears.
Some tears in his heart,
So I let him be my friend.

Unicorn
Edmund Emmett

I found a unicorn in the fire place.

It was elegantly, prancing around and around in the flames.

It stopped suddenly (because out of the window) it saw a bolt of lightning.

I could see the fear in its eyes,

Then it fluttered its wings and rose up the chimney.

I presumed it was going to its home in a magical land far-far away.

I can't believe I witnessed such a thing but I hope the unicorn does come back because I could play a game with him.

Alien in my Closet
Toby Hastings

I looked in my closet where all my clothes should be.
There was something different about it;
One of my toys fell out, so
I picked it up and threw it back inside,
But out it popped again!

I moved one of my biggest toys to one side.
Behind it was something I could not describe;
Some sort of ugly alien making a grunting whine,
A weird creature lurking, threateningly.

Quickly, I picked him up
And lobbed him into the laundry basket.
He curled up very comfortably,
I was tired and I fell asleep; an early start tomorrow.

I wasn't in the best of moods when I heard a cry.
'Aaah! The alien!' I thought.
I sprinted to my window, as if I was Usain Bolt.
I saw the alien running down the street.
I was so upset. That would have been my best
science project yet!

The Golden Eagle
Finn Magee

I jump on a bus with my dad in broad daylight.
We climb up the stairs and start talking.
Two giant claws rip the windows and give me a fright.
I hear a loud noise. Is it a screech or squawking?

The bus lifts abruptly off the ground.
Swaying side to side, we rise to the sky.
Suddenly we're spinning and rotating rapidly around.
We get higher and higher as we fly.

I think it's a massive flock of seagulls,
But then I catch a glimpse of gold.
It's an eagle, a giant eagle …
Who will believe me if this story is told?

A Tiger in my House
Kara Mapstone

I found a tiger in my house,
It was trying to kill a very small mouse.
I looked at the tiger, I blinked and blinked.
It wasn't black and orange, it was bright pink!

I'd never seen one before,
And then I noticed his steel paw.
This was getting very strange.
I thought I should put him in a cage.

His ears were poking up at me.
I think he was a bit hungry.
I gave him food and a drink.
He picked it up with a clink.

His wet, black nose twitched.
He looked at me like a witch.
He was looking at me, his eyes were red.
I had to go before I was dead.

The Centaur in the Music Store Room
Sam Shepherd

I found a centaur in the music store room.

Must have come from the caves,

For he is covered in soil and dust.

I fed him on pistachios and the rays of the sun.

I took him and set him free,

But the next day,

He was back again!

He made a nest of cello cases,

Which he put behind the drums.

He made a pillow of music bags.

He played with this day and night.

I am so amazed to have seen him,

For he is the finest creature ever.

But you will only see him,

If you believe in him.

Rocket in my Pocket
Toby Millar

I was walking along,
When I started to fly.
My immediate thought was,
'I'm going to die!'

As I shot towards the moon,
I realised,
'I'm not going to be home soon.'

The reason was, I clung to a rocket
That I had picked up
And put in my pocket.

I put my hand into my pocket
To hide a jam tart,
And accidentally pressed
The button marked 'start'.

The wind howled by
As I flew through the air.
I clung to my rocket thinking,
'This isn't fair!'

It felt like a dream,
But then I saw the mayor,
Staring up at me.
Did he dare?

Oh what they will say?
Oh what shall I do?
If I don't get back
For English period two!

Night Fears
Daniel Stacey

In amongst my toys,

I sometimes hear a noise.

It happens in the middle of the night.

Startled, I jump up.

I listen to see if it comes again.

I hear a quiet, rustling sound.

I'm sweating, quivering with fear

As I tip-toe silently across my creaky floor

Towards my toys.

Slowly, I reach into the box

And my hand touches ...

The rough bumps of lego bricks,

The smooth, rubbery wheels of my remote control car

And the soft fur of my warm, comforting teddy.

I snatch him up

And rush back to my cosy bed,

Heaving the covers over my head.

I feel safe.

Street Cries
Orla Tann

I work on a games stall

I am a young girl that helps on a stall.
Come and get games, large and small.
Games with monsters and a scary bear.
Games to hog; games to share.

'Buy your games!' called The mayor

Buy your games!
Come get your games and meet with the mayor.
He's vile and vicious and not very fair.
Buy your games!
He cheats as much as he is able.
He kicks your knees under the table.
Buy your games!

Elephant in my Kitchen
Christopher Straughan

There's an elephant in my kitchen,

I don't know what to do!

There's an elephant in my kitchen,

Just escaped from the Zoo.

There's an elephant in my kitchen,

That's drunk all of the juice.

It's eaten all the chocolate mousse,

And now it's on the loose.

There's an elephant in my kitchen,
That's eaten all the food.
It's eaten all the bread and cheese,
And now I'm in a mood.

There's an elephant in my kitchen,
It's knocked over some soup.
It's nesting in the fruit,
And jumping through the roof!

There was an elephant in my kitchen,
That's gone to the Zoo to rest.
There was an elephant in my kitchen,
That left me all this mess.

I saw an Ostrich
Emma Sykes

I saw an ostrich on the wall
She must have been ten feet tall.
Her big long feet gripped the wall
Her face was very bare and small.

How she got there I do not know.
She may have flown from her foe.
I'll find out later because I've got to go.
I guess it's something I'll never know.

I next saw the ostrich in the mall.
I think she was more than ten feet tall.
She definitely wasn't very small
And she was playing with her special ball.

How she got there I do not know.
She may have flown from her foe.
I'll find out later because I've got to go.
I guess it's something I'll never know.

I then saw the ostrich in a ball,
Rolling it around looking quite cool,
But having some quite nasty falls.
Making her look like a fool.

How she got there I do not know.
She may have flown from her foe.
I'll find out later because I've got to go.
I guess it's something I'll never know.

Next I found her in my hall.
I thought I was becoming quite a fool
Seeing her, and all in all,
It was driving me crazy and up the wall.

How she got there I do now know,
But sorry now I've got to go.
I'll come back later so you can know,
What happened to my ostrich, Flo.

A Small Pterodactyl
James Taylor

There's a pterodactyl in
my basement.
It rested overnight, and gave me
a big fright.

I tried it with a triple decker
cheeseburger fresh from KFC.
The pterodactyl spat it all over
the floor and it was quite a mess
for me!

The pterodactyl was going to rest.
So it made a nest.
As a guest, the pterodactyl deserved
to rest.

The next morning, I looked in my
Wonderful basement and ...
He had gone!

Elf in a Drawer
Jemima Tollworthy

I found an elf sleeping in my drawer.
He was the tiniest man that I ever saw.
He'd made himself a toasty-warm nest
From an old pair of socks and a tatty, red vest.

My jaw fell open, but before I could speak
He opened one eye and let out a shriek.
I backed away slowly then gave him a smile.
He seemed to calm down after a while.

I pulled up a chair and together we sat,
Chatting for ages about this and that.
He wanted to stay living here in my room,
'Till the next elf festival, later in June.

I gave him chocolate and cookies for tea.
He was so very nice and kind to me.
He's a really nice elf and he's super-bright
Now he does my homework every night!

A Monster in my Bedroom
Oscar Wills

I've found a monster in my bedroom.
I think it must have come from a cave
Because it's muddy and smelly.
I think it might be hungry.

It fed on many things;
The roots of a plant, a magazine
And a laptop,
But it seemed to sigh each time.

Nothing was quite right,
Until I gave it some bark;
It munched and chomped
And seemed to smile with every bite.

I put it in a tree to rest,
In a very comfy nest,
But it climbed down
And was snoring a minute later in *my* bed!

I Found a Fish, a Dog and a Cat
Natalie Wigfield

I found a fish with shimmering scales.
It flipped under my bedroom door
And rolled across my wooden floor.
I was shocked to see it lying there,
Suffocating, spluttering,
Gasping, gurgling.

I found a dog with a soft, silky coat.
It was hunting rabbits in the field
And rolling in the wet mud.
I was delighted to see it running wildly,
Chasing, racing,
Leaping and lively.

I found a cat with ginger fur.
It was lurking in the playground.
I heard it purr and went to investigate.
I was happy to see it licking its paws,
Curling up in a ball.
Then, eyes tight shut
It dozed in the warm sun.

Year 6. Mr Innes' Set
Taking a Trip Back to 1939

This term we have travelled back to Britain in the Second World War by reading *Goodnight Mr Tom* by Michelle Magorian.

Through role play, drama and creative writing we have explored what it was like to be evacuated from the city to the countryside. We read original accounts from real-life evacuees and found out what it was like to be separated from family and friends and to be placed with strangers in the countryside.

Most evacuees had a warm welcome and a happy time, like William Beech in *Goodnight Mr Tom*. However, life wasn't quite as nice for an unlucky few.

In the letters and diaries we created, we imagined ourselves as very different characters and put ourselves into their shoes. We hope that you too will enjoy reading about life in 1939 and will see the countryside through the eyes of those children who escaped the Blitz there.

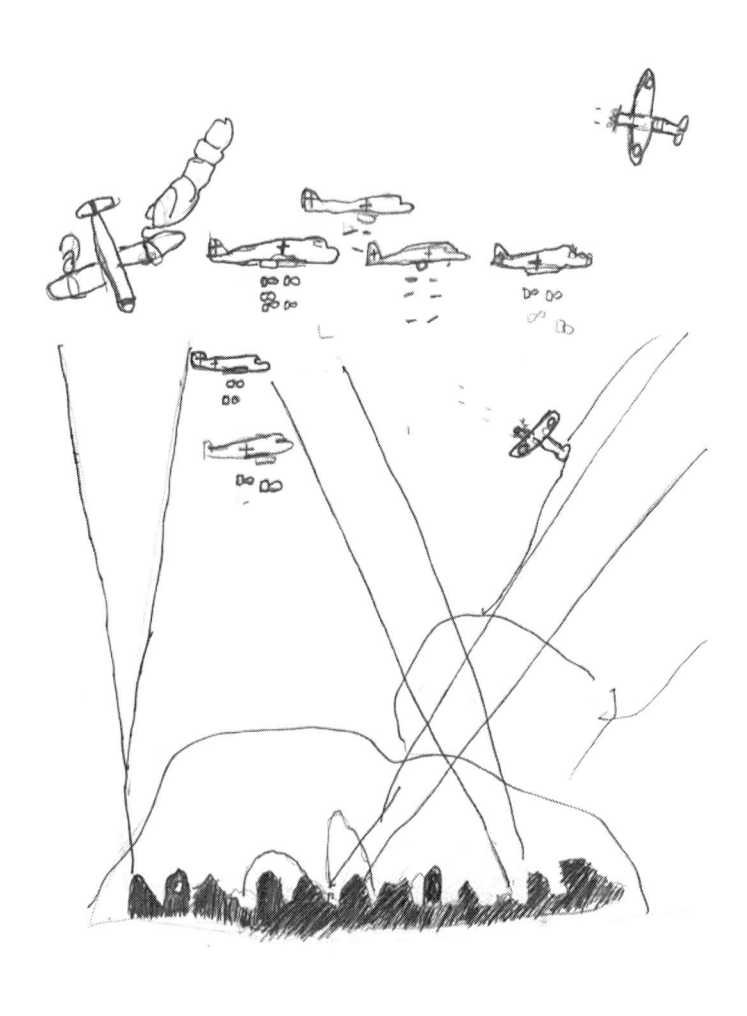

Illustration by Evan Watson

Escapee in the Making
Boris Adams

The warehouse was a ruined wreck. The door was locked but that did not stop me. I found a huge, gaping hole in the wall, dripping with some horrible, slimy moss. I stepped through it. The warehouse was a dump. There were rotting wooden crates and clumps of dripping moss hung on the ceiling.

Rank. That was the word I would use to describe the horrible smell. It smelled like a carcass being devoured by vultures. I gagged. The sun was setting behind the clouds and dark purple rays coated the warehouse, casting shadows over the wall. At this time Mister Garrick would shout at me to get the firewood.

I shuddered. I would give anything to be away from that horrible shack. Darkness settled over Clovelly. I bent down and fell over, the marks on my legs aching with a dull throb. Memories scuttled up from the deep of my mind. I rushed to the past, remembering the beatings, remembering the night I ran away. My legs buckled and the floor rushed towards me.

When I woke up, I saw the rotting wood above me

and the moss hanging down. I got up off the floor and went over to the broken wall. I looked over the rubble and saw a fishing boat, docked at the port. A crazy idea surfaced in my mind; I might just be able to jump aboard the small boat and hopefully stay in hiding until it left, then I would be free.

Early in the morning, I crept down to the dock. The boat was old and rusty. The blue paint peeled off in strips, but I could just make out the faded name, 'The Old Hopeful'.

The Diary of an Evacuee
Tristan Antcliff

Today is the end of my first week at the farm in Devon.

Tom asked me to milk the cow and so I went to find it. I was fascinated, looking at the cow, until I dropped the bucket, which made the cow go, 'Moo'. I ran back inside, frightened. Tom realised he hadn't shown me how to milk the cow, so he demonstrated how to squeeze some sausage-shaped objects, which were teats, and milk squirted out. That was how I learnt to milk a cow.

I was told to go and shovel some horse poo into the pile. I dropped the spade and the horse went, 'Neigh,' so I ran away again, feeling scared out of my skin.

Tom started laughing for some reason. He showed me that there was nothing to be scared of. I walked along with a wheelbarrow full of horse manure and tipped it into the pile. The foul, toxic gases made my head spin. Then I must have fainted.

Thank goodness Tom found me. He washed the stuff from my eyes. The water he'd used was now murky brown, the colour of a dark oak tree.

The next day Tom asked me to round up the sheep into the next field. It ended up with the sheep chasing *me*, with me running for my life into the other field.

That night I thought about why Tom had found all that I had done so funny and the only reason I came up with was that he had never seen anyone who was scared of animals before.

Tom stopped giving me jobs that included animals. I wonder why?

Jerry the Boarder
Oscar Bowker

Dear Mummy,

I am writing to say I like it at boarding school. The people here are nice and so are the mistresses.

If I get a piece of blotting paper, a pen and some writing paper, I can tell you how I am feeling. I miss you so. I can't wait till the Blitz is over and I can come back to London and see you.

My best friend Andrew and I have been doing our homework together – but not copying. We are roommates. Thank you so much for my new fountain pen; it makes writing more comfortable. At the moment I am doing hard spellings like *said*, *friend* and *massive*.

I hate Miss Anny. She is my Geography teacher. Today I put itching powder and custard in her gym knickers. If you think she is bad, she is three times worse than that. I think I may die, her lessons are so boring!

Miss Anny gave Andrew the slipper. That's what made me angry enough to put itching powder and custard in her underwear. Soon she will find out it was me but I don't care! She can feel the pain

Andrew had to have.

    Is Daddy alright in London?

    I love it here at boarding school.

    I will send you another letter soon.

Love,

Jerry XOXO

Letter to Mama
Charlotte Darvill

> Rose Cottage
> Buxton Lane
> Marshfield
> CD2 8OP
> 10th July 1940

Dear Mama,

I'm at a farm. I'm being treated well; they have made me very comfortable and at home. I love the beds, rest assured, Mama. It is all a new experience.

The animals are strange and noisy. When I first heard them it gave me a shock. It is alright now they have explained to me what a sheep and a cow are. There is a really nice dog called Eleanor. We have made great friends and have lots of cuddles. She has big floppy ears, soft yellow fur and a really cute name tag.

On Monday we went apple picking in the orchard. The apples were all very juicy and sweet. They were different colours - red, green and some both colours – and the trees' leaves were orange, yellow, green and red.

That night for tea we had pork, from pigs on the

farm, apple sauce and apple juice. All of the sweet and sour tastes in your mouth – yum!

Well, there are two girls on the farm. They are alright, I suppose. Their names are Agnes and Elsie. I've tried giving them my bracelets and clothes.

I have been to school and it is all great. I learnt my ABC yesterday. To be honest, it is all a bit too easy. I have met lots of new friends including a really nice girl called Phoebe. She has brown wavy hair, a tweed jacket, blue shorts, a flower top and shiny boots. My form teacher is Miss Chin. She is lovely and kind. If you are good, she gives you a sweet treat. If you are naughty, you get a smack.

Take care of yourself.

Lots and lots of love,

Emma xxxxxxx

Letters Home
Alby Davies

The Train

10th of October 1940

Dear Mother,

I am writing to make sure you are not missing me and to say thank you for the sherbet lemons. They taste like sunshine in my mouth. I am on the train playing cards with Harry and Ben (my new friends). I met them boarding the Underground. It was dark and stuffy down there. Chaos!

We have just gone past a white, fluffy animal called a sheep. Apparently it is what my jumper is made from – wool! This is the first time I've seen a sheep in real life, although I've looked at them in books before at school. I can also see golden fields with red tractors. They are harvesting the wheat.

I hope that Miss White (the Billeting Officer) finds me a nice family to stay with. I will write again when I know the address I am staying at.

Yours truly,

Albert

Letter from an Evacuee
Corbin Hunter

Dear Mummy,

I am writing to you from school because my tutor said it would be a nice thing to do after all this time apart. I feel very safe here. I hope you are too.

The people I am staying with are very rich; they have a big house and a pet squirrel, called Jerry! A squirrel is an animal with fur all over it, a bit like a teddy. They are red or grey, have a duster on their rear and are addicted to nuts.

I am staying with a boy called Tom. We were made to clean the toilet because we were rather bold. Since Tom is quite a small boy, he fell in the toilet! I think he needs to eat more or it may happen again, and we will get into a lot more trouble. He is from another city in England called Bristol.

In school we are learning plurals in spelling and when I return I usually help with milking the cows. The countryside is a lot bigger than the city and smells different and is a lot quieter.

I hope you are doing well.

Lots of love,

Corbin X

Rose's Letter
Eleanor Graham

Rocket Cottage

Salarard

Cotswolds

England

30th August 1939

Dear Mother,

I will start with the bad news and that is I have been split up from William, my dear brother. We could not stay together because the family could only keep one child and they chose me. I am now going to tell you some good news. The family I am staying with are the Bumbles – Mr Bumble, Mrs Bumble, Lily Bumble and Joseph Bumble.

They are rich, very lovely and kind. They have a big house and give me food two times a day. They send me to school and I have my lunch there.

But at school there's this girl called Daisy. She's French. She thinks she's the Queen but I think she's a spoilt brat. Her parents buy her toys every day and she gets picked up by her nanny in a posh horse and cart. Daisy waves goodbye to us and says, 'Goodbye, losers.'

After school Lily and I run back to her house, go to the garden and play on the seesaw. When we have finished doing that we run round the garden and then we go in for tea. It is great living with the Bumbles – I have learnt so much; there was this strange animal in the garden and they said it was a hedgehog. This is how I describe it: a small brown creature with a black shiny nose that goes up and down. On its back it has a brown scrubbing brush. Every time you go near it, the bristles on the brush get longer. Its small legs are like flippers and they have four of them. Another thing I know about these strange animals is that they are mammals.

I have also learnt to count all the way up to one hundred and for a girl of eight that is quite an achievement.

That is all I really wanted to tell you. Hope you are well. See you soon?

Yours lovingly,

Rose Mitchell

An Unpleasant Stay
Tom Hocking

>Farm House
>Copse Farm
>Little Slopsbury
>Somerset
>Monday 18th September 1939

Dear Mummy,

I am living in a place without any noise and with a very peculiar smell. I am staying with a 'f-a-r-m-e-r' who talks funny. He lives surrounded by things he calls fields and animals. There is one that is black and white and has a sack hanging from its belly. It is called 'Daisy'. There are also animals that eat slop and spend all day in mud.

Conversations with the farmer are always very short because he says things like, 'Ooh-ar, that 'ere's me sheep dog.' In fact the other day, the farmer said, 'You 'ere go 'n' 'et the cows ready for milking.'

So I went into one of the fields and realised that the farmer was mad; milk comes from the grocery store. I stood there feeling awfully lost. The cows were giving me the evil eye so I started to back away, but I slipped on cowpats and fell flat on my back and stayed there until the farmer's wife found me.

Now, putting poo, the farmer's speech and fields aside, I can get onto the more serious point: save me from this pit of poor hygiene and hay! I've only been here for five days but, as each smelly day goes by, I get madder and madder. I much prefer it in London where the only noises are banging, shouting and engines.

I might have gone off me rocker already, so SAVE ME FROM THIS MUDDY, FLUFFY, MAD, HAY-CHEWING PLACE! It might already be too late. Help me!

Yours sincerely,

Tom X

Rosemary's Letter
Hannah Medley

>Chixall Cottage
>Blossom-on-the-Water
>England
>29th of August 1940

Dearest Mother,

I am writing to you to tell you about my life as an evacuee. At the moment I live with the Angwarla family. They have two girls, Nancy and Ruth, both younger than me, and one boy, Joseph, who is older.

I am really enjoying my life in the country. It is a new experience. I have started school at Blossom-on-the-Water Junior School. I have made lots of new friends and have been learning my numbers (which is way too easy). There is this girl called Alice and she is the teacher's pet. All she does all day is go around telling the entire staff of the school how much she likes them. My teacher, Mrs Chaberry, is on the bad side of good; if you are good she is kind, if you are bad she can lose her temper very easily.

On Saturday evening I went for a walk in the woods and spotted a very strange creature. It was black and white striped. It smelled absolutely awful. Its eyes were tiny and stared at me like I was an odd something from a different land. Its pink, wet nose was snuffling in the leaves. According to Mr Angwarla it was a badger. What a name to call a disgusting little thing like that!

On Friday, in gas mask practice, I made fun of Alice by saying she looked like a badger. She told the teacher and within a second I found myself in the headmistress' office. I have to admit it was funny!

In their cottage I have my own bed and room. Mr and Mrs Angwarla treat me to hot water and clean facilities but I really miss being home with you. Mrs Angwarla is an amazing cook. Yesterday she made us toad-in-the-hole. So basically I am really enjoying it!

So to round it all up, I am really missing you and please could you write back. See you soon.

Yours sincerely,

Rosemary

Sian Framsy – The Diary
Luci Mitchell

Friday 10th 1941

Dear Diary,

Today I was made to muck out the stables. It was disgusting! Mam'selle Fig made me do the dirty work because she's too posh and 'ladylike' to do it. She's a bossy and mean woman!

She's about as bad as I expected. In fact she's worse. I've already tried to escape three times and got it in the neck every time: three slashes and then put in the cage.

No-one wants to go in the cage. It's the place where she keeps her rat. She says she found it in the garden but I bet she bought it just for me! I'm scared not of her (well I am) but of all the feathery things that run around the place, like a dog on the run.

She's rich but doesn't share any of her luxuries with me. I used to read fairy tales – how there was a happy ever after – but I'll probably die if she keeps on beating me and not feeding me.

I secretly go and eat from the pigsty after dinner. It's better than nothing.

There are two other people who live here called

Agatha and Cristobel. They are actually really nice. I think they're just glad to have someone else their age around here. I mean, it's quite a lonely village.

I have to walk seven miles in the morning – every day – to school, while they get taken on a horse drawn carriage (their father is the Mayor).

Whenever their mother makes them do something horrible to me, like hitting me, they do it, but only do a fake one. They're very kind.

I'm going to sit down and write a letter to mother – if I survive!

Dear Mother and Father
Ellie Mount

Dear Mother and Father,

I am writing to you just to tell you how I am, living on the farm with Mr and Mrs Baker. It's nothing like living at home with you, Daisy and George. I have to get up very early to milk the cows and feed the chickens before going to the local school.

Mr and Mrs Baker have no children but they do have another evacuee. Her name is Ivy. She is very small and scruffy and carries her teddy around the farm. Mr and Mrs Baker are horrible to me and Ivy. You wouldn't believe how many whip marks they have given me. By the way, thank you so much for that beautiful necklace from Tahiti, but Mrs Truncheon took it away because it's not school uniform.

Mrs Truncheon is my teacher. She's horrible, especially to me, and she looks like a witch with warts all over her face. She is teaching me to read but it's completely impossible. Have you ever heard of subtraction? Apparently it's a maths thing and it's my homework but Mr and Mrs Baker won't help me either. They believe you only learn if you do it by yourself, which I think is completely stupid!

I have been trying to run away from here but I can never find the perfect time. I have tried, but they keep finding me. I wish I could come back to London. Living on the farm here just isn't the same. I wish this stupid war would end.

My friend Julia, from school, has invited me to go to the music hall with her. I would love to go but I doubt Mr and Mrs Baker will let me.

I am extremely scared that a bomb will come down and hit me. I have a gas mask and I am being taught how to use it, but I am awful at it. I miss you so much and hope to see you soon.

Lots of love,

Your loving daughter, Jane xx

The Escape
Jonathan Otoide

The first day I came here it looked alright, but now I have seen how gruesome life is in the countryside.

I was a Manchester boy living in the middle of Somerset. I saw a lot of new animals - cows, chickens and pigs - because my new home was on a farm. Cows were very peculiar to me at first because they make milk from under their body. I loved teasing the animals but they didn't talk back.

My hosts always managed to make me do the dirty work, like mucking out. It smelled toxic and left me smelling like a pig. All my clothes stank of animal waste.

Two other evacuees lived there with me. One boy was called Brett and the other was Albert. They were nice I suppose, or at least Brett was.

My hosts tried to be nice and there was hot water, but they gave us strange food to eat. I tried running away once, but that left a lot of marks on my body. I planned to try again, though.

Finally, the day I was going to escape came round. I woke up in the middle of the night, ready for my getaway. For some reason I felt as if someone was watching me, but it was just me at the door.

I sprinted out of the old house into the mist. I ran even faster than I had before. This was also further than I'd ever got before.

But then something really, really bad happened to me. Just when I thought I had made about enough distance without having a heart attack, I bumped into something hard in the darkness. I fell over. Stars started spinning around my head and everything went black.

When I woke up I had a fright, as I saw someone looking over me.

'You look lost, pet,' she said in a Manchester accent. 'I think you could do with a new owner.'

The Evacuee Who Ran Away
Fleur Smailes

The whipping, the red hot pokers. The slaving: they treated me like I was a nine-year-old skivvy. The filth I had to pick up.

I could just hear her voice screaming at me, telling me, 'Naughty boy! Naughty boy!'

I missed my mum, my loving mum who would hug me every night and say, 'I love you,' and I didn't appreciate it. She was probably dead by now.

I wished I had spent more time with her.

And there I was, running away from a horrid childhood. What should I do? I just wanted to run home but I knew the war was going on and I would have nowhere to stay. Well, that's why we got sent here, wasn't it?

Anyway, I needed to find somewhere to sleep. I found a barn and fell asleep very easily in the hay.

I woke up that morning and found a man looking at me. I suddenly closed my eyes. I didn't know where I was, but I didn't want him to know I was awake.

And then I felt him touch me. His hand was warm and very comforting.

He asked me where I had come from and what my name was.

'Tom T-Tom Baker,' I muttered.

He told me to come and explain what had happened, to him and his wife.

I explained the whole story to them and he said he was away from home once and found it very hard too. He said I could live with them, but they had to tell the other family that I was here and safe.

The new family are kind to me and I am having a great time now.

Yesterday, I helped out with the farm and milked the cows, which was fun, and then we had some tasty, warm cocoa.

We have delicious food and their home is lovely. They have a dog called Rufus and he is really, really sweet.

I love my new home.

A Letter from Amelia
Amy Smith

Rose Cottage

Church Road

Cornwall

ZB25 SA8

Thursday 9th September 1940

Dear Mama,

I wanted to write to let you know I am fine. I am staying in a lovely, cosy cottage, with a really kind and thoughtful man called Pete and I am lucky to be here. It's fun but all the time I am thinking of you and hoping you're alright, with the bombing and all that.

Pete lets me sleep in a *bed!* It's certainly more comfy than sleeping under the table in the Morrison shelter! Every morning Pete makes me breakfast, and then I walk across the road to school. It's called Orchard House.

I am enjoying school a lot at the moment. In English we are beginning to write short stories. I find it really fun, but at times a little tricky. There's a girl called Phoebe, who put her name on my story. Mrs Church told Phoebe that it was perfect but she told me off for lying when I said it was mine. She said I had to learn when to stop.

It is really quiet down here, and all I ever hear are birds singing away in the trees and villagers' whistling. It is really shocking for me that there aren't any air raid sirens or the sound of bombs dropping down.

I would love to hear from you soon.

By the way, this morning when Pete and I went for a walk in the fields I saw this big, black and white creature. It made really strange noises, like a wolf howling on the night of a full moon. I was petrified! I clung onto Pete's sleeve but he just laughed at me and said there was nothing to worry about and it was just a cow. I felt really silly after that. I'm missing you loads!

Take care of yourself,

Amelia X

P.S. I would love for you to come and visit me sometime.

P.P.S. What should I do about Phoebe?

The Telegram
Emma Thomas

On the day George arrived on the train, there was something smelly wafting through the air. He shuddered and walked on down the lane.

As he glimpsed the place he was going to stay, he felt horrified. He looked around the yard and saw four black and white creatures. They were enormous and had fat rippling under their skin.

George stepped forward, noticing how dark the house looked. The man who opened the door was not welcoming.

'Come in,' he said, 'I'm Mr Trein.'

The place was full of what George hated most: filth. The farmhouse had three small rooms and slime spreading down the walls. He breathed in, cautiously.

George was lucky that there were two beds in the house; he shared one with two other boys and Mr Trein slept in the other.

As George lay in bed, he thought for the hundredth time, 'You need to escape. Mr Trein is horrible and life isn't ever going to be good here.'

Each day, George got up reluctantly.

One morning, he walked around the room to the window. He'd already been here for a week now and still hated it; apart from being with the two boys it wasn't any fun. George looked outside and saw a man wearing blue clothes. He was placing a blue envelope and a box on the doorstep.

When George came downstairs, Mr Trein had brought them in.

'George, come here. I've got some bad news for you,' he said. 'Look.'

On the letter it said 'Telegram' and in the box there were medals.

Tears fell down George's face as he realised that his dad was dead. He opened the box and looked at the medals: Bravery, Strength, Courage, Respect. A note inside said, 'He always fought for freedom and good.'

'Now,' George thought. 'Time to escape to freedom, to London, and to live a normal, happy life, free from the filth. Time to get home.'

The Story of an Evacuee
Evan Watson

It all started in London, 1939. When the first bomb raid hit us, it was so frightening. People thought the Blitz was a punishment from God, but I think it's the work of men of the devil. It was the worst thing I can remember about the war. I think this was a lesson; this is what changed my life. There was two weeks of chaos, then the government made a decision to send children to the countryside.

I went to my Uncle Steven's. I don't like Uncle Steven. He really isn't nice; sometimes he hits me while mum's not in the room, but I went there with my family.

The journey to Tisbury by motorcar was so long, I ended up sleeping in the car, which was difficult because of the sound the thing makes. At my uncle's, life was so different to home. Uncle Steven's house was huge, twice as big as ours, and I thought that was big. He also had quite a big farm.

Once, the cows escaped and we all had to help, even my sister who can't stand cows. Apart from us they were the most precious thing on the farm.

One night, when I was lying in bed, I could see

light coming from under the curtain and the loud bangs kept me awake. I looked behind the blackout blinds and saw Salisbury on fire. Planes, in their thousands, were flying over. The Spitfires were there, trying to defend the town. I had never seen them in action before.

I could see planes falling from the sky, spinning downwards towards the ground. This wasn't the only time; it happened quite a lot. I never forgot that night; I remembered my friends from school and hoped that they were all alive.

Life was never boring as four years went by. When it was time to go, it felt like I was leaving my home behind.

I remember London looking like a dump when I returned, buildings collapsed in every street.

An Evacuee's Letter
Imogen Smith

> Lanny Manor
> Wicombe Lane
> Marshfield
> 11th October 1939

Dear Mama,

Thank you for the clothes, bracelets and photos of us together. The family are lovely and they have even signed me up for the local sewing club. Mr and Mrs Thompson live in the Cotswolds.

Mrs Thompson makes sticky toffee pudding every Sunday. The farm animals are friendly and the daughter of Mr and Mrs Thompson has taught me how to ride a horse. The boy who helps on the farm is stuck up and really chatty and boring.

When I first arrived all I saw was poo. I refused to get out of the car and get my pink painted leather pumps dirty and covered in mud. I just wish I could have Nana looking after me. I really miss her. Do you know if she is alright? Is she living with you?

I am thinking of you dearly.

Love,

Sue Mainly X

Illustration by Boris Adams

Year 6. Mrs Heaney's Set
Truth or Tale?

Welcome to a pastiche of creative writing inspired by the novel *A Pack of Lies* by Geraldine McCaughrean.

The imaginative stories embedded within the main plot of this novel have roused the curiosity of our Year 6 students. After each tale, based upon an interesting object in Mrs Povey's Antiquary, we are left wondering, truth or lies?

As a result, Year 6 have responded with their own truths and tales inspired by objects in their homes. We hope you enjoy our contribution and challenge you to decide whether we ourselves have become, A Pack of Liars!

Illustration by Guy Willcock

Illustration by Isaac Fee

The Dolphin Mug
Rory Akbar

It was a stormy night on the Holy barge, and the captain was drinking out of his favourite mug topped up with beer. He walked out of his quarters and went on deck to see the crew. He slipped, dropped the mug into the sea and lay on the deck watching the beer slip down through the cracks.

'NO! My precious mug!' he wailed.

The mug was given to the captain as a gift twenty years ago when he first became a sailor. It was his lucky mug which he always took on voyages. He believed the mug gave him good luck and kept him safe from the evil nymphs. His grandfather, the greatest sailor of all time, had been attacked and tortured by them. They cursed the sea upon which he sailed, and when he fell overboard, they burned his ship and made him watch.

A dolphin that was swimming close to the surface picked up the mug. Strangely, the mug which had been plainly decorated while in the hands of the captain was now adorned with sea, seaweed, a fish, and the handle looked like a dolphin, too. The mug was the dolphin's loot now, submerged under the icy sea water.

The mystery behind it may never be discovered.

Lucky Finbar's Obituary
Tallulah Brady

Lucky Finbar was born on Friday 13th 1977. He died on the 31st December 35 years later.

Finbar was a very superstitious man. He had a rough childhood which led to him being this way. He was also very religious and believed strongly in God.

Finbar was born in a small village called Shackleboot in Ireland. His father made a living from keeping and trading horses. Life was good and Finbar was not yet superstitious.

One day he saw a new moon through his window. He knew it was supposed to be unlucky, but he didn't believe in that stuff yet. But the next day tragedy struck. His Mother became incredibly ill and unfortunately died. Finbar did not know what to do or who to blame, so he blamed the new moon. From this day on Finbar was Ireland's most superstitious person.

Finbar grew older and knew he had to make a living, so he got a job as a horse trainer. Finbar had a real talent and became a full-time jockey. However, he was still superstitious.

His career as a jockey was very successful; he

won the Dublin Gold Stakes several times. Everybody put their money on Finbar's horse and they were always right. This made many betting shops go bankrupt.

A fortune teller told Finbar that he would die before the year was out. Finbar believed him. He was driven mad by this. On December 31st Finbar figured that if he could stop the clock he could stop time and, therefore, not die.

With five minutes left to live, Finbar ripped the clock off the wall. His strength and energy were so powerful and the clock was so battered that it fell on Finbar, unfortunately killing him.

Teapot Story
Sam Butters

Once there was a very evil emperor who ruled over China. He took money from his people and if they didn't pay their taxes he would send an assassin to kill them and their family. He had a powerful army which could destroy any country in the world.

One day greed overcame him and he decided he wanted China to himself. He told his army to destroy all the houses, but when the public heard about this they formed their own army to kill the emperor. They broke into his house and spied on him drinking tea from his favourite teapot. One of them jumped out and stabbed him in the back.

***

Five hundred years later, Charles Haddock ducked behind a tree after a narrow escape with some natives who had ambushed him. He was in search of the emperor's treasure. Nobody had ever got near it and if he found it he would be a hero back in England. He looked at his map; he was close.

'Only one more day in this stupid jungle,' he thought.

The next day Charles arrived at the tomb. It was huge. He told himself that he would be the first person to get the treasure and that he'd be rich. He was surrounded by treasure! Suddenly he saw something coming up the stairs towards him. He grabbed the closest thing, a decorative teapot, and ran straight for the door.

Peering over his shoulder, he saw a dead army chasing him as he headed towards the river. He jumped in and tried to swim across to the other side, but the water was flowing too quickly. In order to save himself, he let go of the one piece of treasure he had managed to steal.

That very teapot, found by my grandparents on Brighton Beach, now sits on the mantelpiece at home.

I wonder if it *is* the same teapot which once belonged to the Emperor of China?

Pandora's Box
Grace Coumbe

The box opened and everything went cloudy. It was a very strange mist. Finally when the mist cleared, the child had vanished! The customer was speechless.

The shop owner said, 'Nobody should ever lift the lid; it is too powerful to control. There is a monster in the box called Pandora. She comes out in the mist and kills the person who has disturbed her. Most of the items next to the box are very dangerous as well.'

'What will happen now?' asked the customer, still shocked.

'If you take a look in the box now, because Pandora has gone for a while, you will automatically fall into another world. This has happened only once before,' said the shopkeeper dreamily. 'I will close the shop and then we can go there together.'

They walked over to the box and leaned in just far enough to fall in.

'Aggghhhhh!' they screamed.

The shopkeeper and the customer closed their eyes. They were falling down and down, further and further, to the bottom of a very deep, dark hole!

When they opened their eyes again, they were in a town made of sweets. The sun was an extra-large yellow Smartie and the houses were made of gingerbread. They walked to the edge of sweetie world and then floated up into space where they met some fluorescent pink and green aliens! The aliens half flew and half floated as they went away. The shopkeeper and the customer followed them (because they were very curious about the aliens) to the aliens' home on a planet called Mars.

There were at least two hundred Mars bars and the customer and the shopkeeper gazed hungrily at them. A child sat with the aliens, munching a Mars bar.

The Last Thing Left
Justin Davies

He was awarded it, for great service in the war of South Africa. It was a tea-set, including a blue and white plate signed by Queen Victoria. Now, Jones the Spy was living a normal life in the year 1954 where he read about the Second World War.

***

Fifty-seven years earlier.
The pillar crashed above his head, inches from the papers he was cradling in his left arm. He sprinted across the quay. Another shot. He could feel the warmth of the bullet as it whizzed past his right ear. He jumped, and landed splay-legged on the deck of the transport. He lifted the assault rifle from the deck and opened fire on the two enemy soldiers. One man went down but the other darted across to a pillar.

The soldier hid behind the pillar, took aim and fired a single shot. The radar was knocked off. Jones had two choices: one – go back to South Africa and face certain death, or two – head back to England and hope they would pick him up on their radar. The choice was obvious; he returned to England safe and sound along with his helmsman.

***

Back in the present day, Jones was reading the paper when he heard a strange noise. It was whistling! Jones knew that sound only too well. He got up slowly, walked stealthily towards the door, wanting to see what was going to kill him. Suddenly there was a flash of light that illuminated the doorway, then nothing.

His house collapsed in a frenzy of explosions. When the firemen came, there was no trace of a body, just a blue and white plate. It had somehow been thrown clear of the detonation.

The plate I took inspiration from was made at Jutland Stanley Pottery, England 1907-1957.

The Plate: Nagasaki
Joshua Dreelan

Far away in Japan, near the city of Nagasaki, a boy, ragged and thin, sat next to perfectly round pond, fishing. Unexpectedly, a young lady came strolling towards him. She was wearing a traditional crimson-red robe. She had long black hair with a faint gleam to it.

'Hello, what's your name?' asked the young lady.

'Hiroy, my name is Hiroy,' said the boy, honestly.

'My name is Jane. Would you like to follow me?' Jane had taken pity on the boy.

'I've got a surprise for you, Hiroy,' said Jane.

'She's quite friendly,' thought Hiroy. 'Ok, what's the surprise?'

'I can't tell you – it's a surprise!'

'Fine. I will go with you.' Hiroy sighed.

So they started walking towards the centre of the village. They stopped outside a pottery shop. Jane opened the door and indicated for Hiroy to enter.

'My surprise is a job offer. If you accept you will be fed and well looked after. All you have to do is make ten china plates and vases every day,' Jane said, enthusiastically.

Hiroy had never had a job or known a mother's love before. He had always had to scavenge for food to eat. So he accepted.

He started his job the next day and as soon as he began making plates and vases he couldn't stop.

His best plate was the first one he ever made. It was beautiful.

Pandora's Box
Mariel Emmerson-Hicks

A blinding light suffused the room. Liz went closer to the box.

'Come on Elizabeth, step inssside side side the box box box,' said a voice.

She ventured nearer and cautiously put her hand in the box.

'Yesss Yesss Elizzzabeth. Come onnn my dearrrr.' Liz climbed inside the box. 'Yessssss yesss yess Elizzzzabeth. Come onnn my dearrrr. Comeee innnn.'

Liz stepped inside the box and started falling, falling, falling, down and down.

(Liz's Point of View)

'Hello my dear girl, I am Pandora and this is MY box!'

The world went black as a burning pain in my back spread over my body.

I saw Pandora kneel before someone

'My lord, my lord,' she cried in a nervous high-pitched voice, 'my lord I beg for mercy. I've got you the long lost child of Chaos.'

The lord growled, 'Yes you got her, you got her all right. Though what did I say: I SAID NOT TO TOUCH HER!' He slapped her across the face. 'You are dismissed.'

Pandora scampered out the room.

'My child,' he said in a sickeningly sweet voice. 'My dearest child. I am Lord Kronos, King of the Titans – Slayer of Uranus and I am about to be the slayer of YOU!' he chuckled darkly.

'Wait,' I said foolishly. 'Aren't you the one who got defeated by Zeus?'

'You will DIE for your insolence!' He raised his scythe and put it to my throat.

He was just about to strike when a man appeared. Kronos dropped his scythe.

'Ccchaos!' he stuttered.

Lord Kronos sped away realising this was a lost battle and Chaos murmured, 'Until next time, Kronos!'

Then Chaos flashed me to my bedroom. The second I touched the mattress I fell asleep!

The Vase
Isaac Fee

'You'll wanna lick that before it drops, Jakey boy,' said a portly woman from behind the hatch.

Jake and Sam were sitting on the rocks next to one of their favourite spots in the world, licking their 'Hedgehog Daily Specials', an ice cream made of Cornish clotted cream dipped in nuts. 'Rosie's Delights' was perched on the clifftop, as pink as strawberry ice cream.

That evening, the boys jumped over the waves on their bodyboards, engulfed in the blue and white skin of the ocean.

'Hey, Jake! There's a cave over there! I'm gonna check it out! You comin'?' asked Sam.

'Yep!' answered Jake. Together they paddled to the vast, rocky cliff. Facing them was an extravagant opening, like an angry monster baring its huge jagged teeth.

'Wow!' they uttered in unison.

Embedded in the damp, algae-covered floor of the cave was a large, dusty vase.

'That's so cool!' whispered Jake.

'Shall we take it home?' asked Sam, nervously.

They grabbed a piece of slate each and started hammering on the rock. As Sam freed the vase, they heard a deep rumbling from above. A shower of rocks fell on them like a thunderous hailstorm, so that they couldn't see their own feet.

Hours later, a deep voice echoed within the cave.

'Um, hello? Anybody here?'

'Y-y-yes?!' stuttered Sam.

'Here's a hole. Can you can squeeze through it?'

'I can't!' yelled Jake.

'I'm just going to make it bigger,' said the voice. The boys realised it belonged to the coastguard.

After a struggle, Jake managed to squeeze through the hole, followed by Sam.

'I'd better get you two home. Your parents are sick with worry!'

On their journey back to shore, Jake and Sam watched the wake of the boat dissolve into the treacle-like sea. The sky was as black as liquorice, with sherbet sprinkled on top. In the ghostly light of the waxing moon, Sam noticed the inscription on the vase.

'That's Great Grandpa's crest!' he said. 'It must belong to him!'

The Royal Egg
Esme Freeman

There once was a poor woman called Marianne who had a daughter and a son called Charlotte and Hamish. They had one hen each, but they didn't lay eggs because they were too young. They lived in a broken, old cottage with a mouldy bath and windows stained with grease. Bugs were scattered in the kitchen and the sink was covered in black gunk. Hamish and Charlotte both slept on the kitchen table, while Marianne slept on a tiny bed in the toilet. They had no sitting room because the roof had caved in, so only half the cottage could be used. The curtains were meant to be snowy-white, but had ended up grey and covered in dust.

One day Marianne said to the children, 'I'm sorry, but if the hens don't lay eggs in the next three days we can't afford to keep them.'

'But we can, Mummy, we really can. One of them will lay an egg and it will be the nicest egg you've ever tasted. You wait and see!' protested Charlotte, who then stormed off and went to see her hen, Omlet.

'Come on, Omlet, you can lay an egg! If you don't we won't be able to keep you! You've got to do it, Omlet!' she said.

One day passed and Omlet showed no interest in laying an egg at all. Hamish's hen, Egglet, didn't even look at the nesting box and Marianne's hen, Princess, just pecked at the weeds. Hamish told Charlotte they would never manage it.

The very next morning Charlotte jumped off the table at five forty-five!

'Charlotte, you woke me up! We still have two hours of sleep!' Hamish complained.

'I'm going to collect the egg, the egg of dreams!' she said.

Charlotte checked under Princess. No egg. Under Egglet. No egg. She carefully slid her hand under Omlet, closing her eyes and biting her lip and there was ... an egg!

Charlotte bolted across the lawn and back into the house with it.

'MUMMY! AN EGG! The very first egg!'

She held up the egg in triumph and danced around the room.

She cradled it like a baby UNTIL ...

The Unsinkable Plate
Will Gatehouse

On April 15th 1912 the unsinkable Titanic sank! We remember this day because our great-great grandparents were on the Titanic.

My great-great grandparents loved dancing and dining on board the luxurious floating palace. My great-great grandma decided she really wanted a memento of her trip and did a very uncharacteristic thing: she stole a china dinner plate! She slipped it under her shawl and took off with it.

They had just got back to their cabin when the ship jolted to a stop. They were told that the Titanic had started to sink, so they had to put on their life jackets and evacuate on deck. They later found out that the ship had hit an iceberg.

My great-great grandma could already feel the ship starting to sink, so she grabbed her plate and ran up on deck with her husband. In all the frenzy she got separated from him and was put into a lifeboat. In front of her eyes, she saw the great Titanic sink. She clutched the plate to her heart as comfort and protection.

Suddenly, without any notice, her lifeboat

capsized, plunging her into the ice cold sea.

A lifeboat went to look for survivors and managed to find her (and the plate)!

She ended up on board the Carpathia.

When she returned to England, she told her daughter the incredible story about the plate.

The Piece of Crockery
Maya House

In the last century, in 1986, there was a girl who went to Brittany on a school trip during the summer holidays. While she was there, she visited Dinan, Dinard, St Malo and various other places.

While she was in Dinan, she went into a little gift shop where she bought a small plate with a picture on it of 'Les Porches' in Dinan. It was for her grandmother.

As she ran her fingers around the plate, the edges were as smooth as silk. A picture was in the centre of the plate, painted in blue on a white background. It felt like an uneven texture in contrast to the smoothness of the edge. On the reverse of the plate was a mark showing that the plate was made in 'Bretagne' (Brittany), France.

When the little girl arrived home she gave the plate to her grandmother, who was delighted with it and displayed it in her living room.

A few years later her Grandmother passed away and the plate got returned back to the now grown-up little girl.

The grown-up girl went on to have a child of her own. Ten years later, her daughter went on her first school trip away to France. While she was there she visited St Malo, and Dinan as well. In Dinan, the child actually sketched the picture of 'Les Porches' that was on the plate her mother had bought back for her grandmother.

On her return home, the little girl showed her mother her sketch of 'Les Porches'.

Her mother was delighted and immediately fetched the plate and told her daughter about its story, going back twenty-seven years.

The Lucky Plate of Ireland
Edie Nelson

Let me tell you the story of the lucky plate of Ireland. It had been passed down through generations of Irish kings. They believed it was magic. Nobody really knew.

The king had only been king for a few years and the plate belonged to him. Before that, it belonged to his father. He took it everywhere with him, to balls, parades and even important meetings!

One day, the king lost his plate. He couldn't find it anywhere. It wasn't under his bed, in the wardrobe or even in the bathtub. His servants searched high and low, but it couldn't be found.

The king had a very important meeting to go to, so he reluctantly stepped into his horse and cart; without his precious plate.

On that journey, a thunderstorm started up and the bridge they had to cross was struck by lightning. The chauffeur urged the horses onwards, but they didn't want to go over it. He whipped the horses harshly and they moved slowly onto the bridge when suddenly ... CRACK!

The bridge fell away, taken by the river below. The cart went first, tumbling down into the water, followed by the horses. The horses just managed to swim across the river but the young king drowned. All because he forgot his lucky plate.

A few days later, his body was found by a fisher-boy. He was welcomed into the city, as he had found their beloved king.

The Jewellery Box
Eoin O'Neill

A flash of bright light briefly lit up the store followed by a gigantanormous bang!

When Elizabeth opened her eyes, she was still in the jewellery shop, but it was deserted and looked as though it had been bombed; as a matter of fact everywhere else looked the same.

She rubbed her eyes and this time, when she opened them, Elizabeth was in a jungle surrounded by a herd of hippopotamuses.

Meanwhile, back in the shop, Grace, Elizabeth's mother was hysterically screaming, 'Liz! Lizzie! Where are you?' to no-one in particular.

'SIT DOWN AND SHUT UP! Then I'll tell you the story of that there box,' said the shopkeeper.

And so he began.

'That box is made from the stone of the planet Elcarxzo; a planet where the beings focus mainly on time and space travel.'

'You mean to say that there are other humans and also L-L-Liz could be a-a-a-anywhere?' interrupted Grace.

'In answer to your first point, mmm well I wouldn't

exactly go far enough to call them *humans*; more weird, manic, deadly humanoids and in answer to your second, no, she should arrive here in ten minutes, forty-nine seconds and twenty-seven milliseconds – by my watch. You will need to grab her and hold on for all you're worth, while I intone the following chant: GRITH GROTH OMNIS RESO.'

So that's how, ten minutes forty-nine seconds and twenty-seven milliseconds later, the shopkeeper came to be yelling, 'Quick, seize her!'

Grace grabbed Elizabeth and held on tight, causing a vortex to open. The shopkeeper then chanted the incantation and threw the box into the vortex.

A number of things happened in this order: the vortex closed, the box disappeared, Elizabeth stayed there and all the people on the street, who had been watching since the flash of light, applauded.

The Plate
Freya Pattemore

Once there was a girl called Zylene, who lived in Europe. Zylene was on her way to the store (even though she was very poor) when she felt a sharp pain in her foot. She knelt down and saw part of a broken plate. It had patterns of branches and leaves and writing around the outside, painted in what looked like silver filament. She turned it over to look at the back. It said in bold lettering: WORLD WAR II.

A man with long chocolate-coloured hair, tied in a low ponytail appeared. He had eyes as green as grass, his nose was fat and bent slightly to the right. He wore a pale blue jacket and trousers.

'You wanna know the story of the plate?' he asked.

'Of course I do!' said Zylene.

By now people had started to gather round to hear the story of the plate.

'Mrs Macall was fourteen when the war started in 1939. When she was seventeen and a half, she volunteered for the Navy and became a code writer. During the war, Mrs Macall painted all the codes on the plates in silver writing. The plates were taken to the families of people whose husbands or fathers were in the war, to let them know that everything was alright.

When one of the plates was being delivered, it slipped out of the box and smashed to smithereens. No-one has ever picked it up or collected it.

Zylene was staring in amazement at the man who had just told the story.

Zylene read the back of the plate out loud so everyone could hear. 'Made by Mrs Macall WWII.'

Zylene is related to me, as I am one eighth French, and this story has been passed down through generations.

Truth or tale?

Plate Story
Guy Willcock

Long ago in the age of lords, ladies and servants, there lived an Italian family, the Clarinnettos. Every year, the Clarinnettos went to their family cottage in the country. It was during one of these holidays that our story takes place.

The family, Papa Clarinnetto, Madre Clarinnetto and their two daughters, Maria and Isabella, were not wealthy but were minor aristocracy. Their servants did not travel with them on holiday. Unfortunately, the herdsman was taken ill on their day of arrival, which meant they would have to look after their own animals.

'I will not do it, I say! I shan't!' shrilled Madre Clarinnetto.

'But who will help me herd the cattle?' answered Papa Clarinnetto.

'I bet Izzy wouldn't mind helping, Papa,' said Maria, and with that, the trio went down to the cattle shed and led the cattle down to the river for a drink.

All was fine until a calf tumbled into the water. Without a moment's hesitation, Maria dived in to save it, her dress billowing in the water. A second later, she broke the surface with the calf over her shoulder. She swam to the side and got out.

'You stupid girl! You have ruined your dress!' screamed her papa, and he whacked her with his stick. 'Sit over there until I say you can move.'

Suddenly a loud 'Moo!' was heard. One cow had wandered into the river and now the others were following it in. The father and Isabella waded in to help. The cows were stuck in weeds and were beginning to panic. Maria just sat there, watching.

Unexpectedly, Papa Clarinnetto was trampled by a panicking cow. He lay motionless in the water, face down, dead.

'Papa! Oh, Papa!' Isabella shrieked, crying. She tried to reach her father, but got stuck in the weeds and then a cow kicked her in the head.

The second victim. And all the while, Maria just sat and watched.

This is the story which my grandmother painted on a plate when she was a little girl. It is a true story, passed down through generations.

The Mystery Box
Hugh Hudson

The box jumped out at the child, startling her. Memories flowed through her head; and all at once the mother, the shopkeeper and the girl landed with a thud on the marble floor. The shopkeeper started to argue menacingly, but the girl and her mother took no notice of him. They just stared and stared.

In front of them towered a giant. They couldn't work out if it had only one eye or if they were imagining things. So many questions travelled through their heads. Where would they go? What would happen? Where were they? Was it a Cyclops?

The girl and her mother started running so fast, they couldn't stop. They didn't know where they were going. They didn't have time to think about that, so they just sprinted on, not daring to turn around.

After a while, the Cyclops' bellowing grew fainter and fainter, until at last it was heard no more. The shopkeeper called to them to stop. 'It's gone,' he shouted.

Terrified, they fell back against a tree. It gave way and they tumbled back into the shop. They were out of danger.

The Biscuit Tin
Isaac Taylor

There once was a biscuit tin maker, called Lin Feng, who made the most beautiful tins. His master was a nasty man whose face turned crimson and veins showed on his neck when he got angry.

One day, Lin made a tin decorated with a story in which a rich man's daughter was forced to marry a man she hated. The story ends with the daughter running away with a poor gardener, never to be seen again. This tin reminded Lin of his own life. He loved his master's daughter, but she was betrothed to a man she hated.

On the day of a pre-wedding celebration, Lin Feng made a special tin to give to his master's daughter. Upon the tin he painted his usual design, but with his own face as the gardener, and master's daughter as the girl. He hoped she would understand the message and come to him.

After an hour he was about to give up, when suddenly his beloved burst in. They ran away into the woods and were never seen again.

Illustration by Guy Willcock

Acknowledgements

This book was the dream-child of Kim Donovan, children's writer and publisher, and our school has been hugely enriched by the whole experience of writing it. We owe her enormous and grateful thanks for the hours of work and the encouragement she has given us. Without her inspiration, this book would not have happened.

Thanks to Liz MacFarlan for following up on the idea and badgering all involved to help to make it into a reality. Thanks are also owed to Stephen Carr, for his IT expertise and calm head and to Nicola Carr, for endless cutting, pasting and chasing-up of material. For her help with the technical side of the cover design, we thank Jude Maguire. We are grateful to Vanessa White, Louise Trezies and Karen Baldwin for casting their editorial eyes over the manuscript.

Thank you to the teaching staff, who motivated and cajoled our pupils into producing some wonderful, creative pieces.

The biggest thank you of all goes to the pupils of King Edward's Junior School; a joy to work with, our children amaze and enthuse us on a daily basis.

Illustration by Maia West

Index of Authors & Illustrators

Year 3 Class 3L

Ned Alcock	3
Jay Bardsley	3
Freddy Blofeld	4
Josie Butters	5
Tobin Bye	6
Zac Grosjean	7
Henry Jones	8
Charlotte Laver	9
Edward Lewis	2, 9
George Lowrie	7
Wilfie Mantell-Jacob	10
Kit McKeever	11
Rory Medley	12
Alfie Myers	13
Megan Pike	1, 14
Douglas Pritchard	11

Year 3 Class 3J

Thomas Moir	15
Jasper Nejad	16
Harvey Newsam	17
Ben Phillips	18
Isobel Reid	19
Freddie Russell	20
Orson Savage	21
Oscar Shonfeld	22, 23
Ben Sim	24
Max Stein	25
Toby Swale	26, 27
George Tinworth	28
Zoe Trezies	29, 30
Harry Tweedale	31
Claudia Williams	32
Elise Withey	33, 34

Year 4 Class 4R

Harry Adams	37
Anastasia Andreou	38
James Bassil	40

Erica Baxter	41
Ruairi Brady	43
Max Brine	44
Angus Cannock	45
Wilf Clark	47
Alastair Claydon	49
Max Dennis	36, 51
Charlotte Digney	53
Cameron Finnigan	35, 55
Maxim Hagan	57
Stuart Hearn	58
Emma Hocking	59
Rafee Jabarin	61
Kaillash Karthikeyan	63
Cecily Likeman	64
Jack Lintern	65
Lottie Litherland	67

Year 4 Class 4M

Luke Botterill	71
Fabian Drew	73
Tilly Lyons	75, 110
Ophelia Mantell-Jacob	77, 109
Charlie McGuire	79
Noah Nejad	81
Max Newark	83
Scarlett Newsam	70, 85, 110
Gil Nowak	87
Joseph Reece	89
Amelie Rodriguez-Cobham	69, 91
Tristan Rouviere-Hyde	92
Vish Senthil Kumar	94
Luke Smith	95
Jacob Spooner	97
Sheev Tirbhowan	99
Ben von Arx	101, 110
Maia West	103, 109
George White	105, 109
Daniel Wigfield	107

Year 5. Mrs Hardware's English Set

Tanya Ahmed	111, 113
Tom Bertinet	115
Daisy Collett	117
Chris Donovan	119
Olivia Fee	121
Christopher Godwin	123, 167
Theo Laver	125
Lollie McKenzie	127
Ben McNab	129
Joshua Moir	112, 131
Rohan Patil	133
Freddy Purcell	135
Ryan Schumaker	137
Olivia Seaton	139
Sophie Swale	141
Sam Trezies	143

Year 5. Mrs Heaney's English Set

Sebastian Crow	147
Kate Daniels	149
Alex Done	151
Felix Fountain	152
Hannah Gatehouse	153
Lily Grosjean	154
John Lowrie	155
Adi Mishra	156
Arthur Pease	157
Albert Perry	158
Ella Reece	160
James Reid	161
Jacob Robertson	162
Jack Ruddock	163
India Sanderson	164
Isobel Smith	146, 165
Florence Stockham	166

Year 5. Mr Innes' English Set

Matthew Barclay	169
Oliver Brook	171
Ben Dryden	173
Theo Hagan	167, 175

Ebony Hammond	177
Evie Handel	179
Iyshea Hender	181
Luke Hepworth	183
Izzy Hughes	185
Roxy Livingstone	187
Jim McAllister	189
Jack McGladdery	191
Adrian Moayedi	193
Kathleen Nicholas	195
Filip Oczko	197
Conrad Perry	199
Oscar Rudd	201
Aoi Seiki	203

Year 6. Mr MacFarlan's English Set

Mr MacFarlan	207
Phoebe Aisher	208
Orlando Alford	206, 209
Sophie Bassil	210
Adam Baxter	211
Elsie Berry	212
John Claydon	213
Thomas Crawford	214
Alex de Beer	215
Max Entwisle	216
Cecilia Gerber	217
Ammar Hassan	218
Cameron Kelly	219
Megan Lintern	220
Lily Page	205, 221
William Pinder	222, 226
Wilfred Saumarez-Smith	223
Max Sears	224
Alex Weimar	225

Year 6. Mrs Hardware's English Set

Emma Botterill	229
Edmund Emmett	230
Toby Hastings	231
Finn Magee	232
Kara Mapstone	233

Toby Millar	235
Sam Shepherd	234
Daniel Stacey	237
Christopher Straughan	239
Emma Sykes	241
Orla Tann	238
James Taylor	243
Jemima Tollworthy	228, 244
Natalie Wigfield	246
Oscar Wills	245

Year 6. Mr Innes' English Set

Boris Adams	249, 280
Tristan Antcliff	251
Oscar Bowker	253
Charlotte Darvill	255
Alby Davies	257
Eleanor Graham	259
Tom Hocking	261
Corbin Hunter	258
Hannah Medley	263
Luci Mitchell	265
Ellie Mount	267
Jonathan Otoide	269
Fleur Smailes	271
Amy Smith	273
Imogen Smith	279
Emma Thomas	275
Evan Watson	248, 277

Year 6. Mrs Heaney's English Set

Rory Akbar	283
Tallulah Brady	285
Sam Butters	287
Grace Coumbe	289
Justin Davies	291
Joshua Dreelan	293
Mariel Emmerson-Hicks	295
Isaac Fee	282, 297
Esme Freeman	299
Will Gatehouse	301
Maya House	303
Hugh Hudson	313

Edie Nelson   305
Eoin O'Neill   307
Freya Pattemore   309
Isaac Taylor   315
Guy Willcock   281, 311, 316

Illustration by Luke Smith

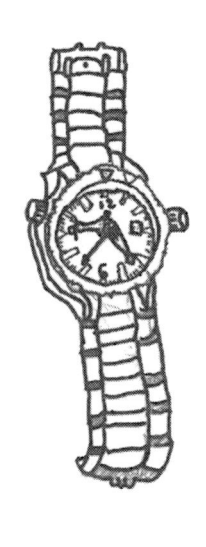

Illustration by Wilfred Saumarez-Smith

Illustration by Charlotte Digney